T0163182

PENGUIN BOOKS
LEAP OF FATE

Jansen Lim is the author of two fiction novels: *The Ties That Bite* and *In Rio You Love a Little More*. His essays and feature articles have appeared in a range of publications from travel and lifestyle magazines to *The Straits Times*. He has also worked as a global project manager, lecturer, and videographer, and he lives in Singapore.

Leap of Fate

Jansen Lim

PENGUIN BOOKS

An imprint of Penguin Random House

PENGUIN BOOKS

USA | Canada | UK | Ireland | Australia
New Zealand | India | South Africa | China | Southeast Asia

Penguin Books is part of the Penguin Random House group of companies
whose addresses can be found at global.penguinrandomhouse.com

Published by Penguin Random House SEA Pte Ltd
9, Changi South Street 3, Level 08-01,
Singapore 486361

Penguin
Random House
SEA

First published in Penguin Books by Penguin Random House SEA 2024

Copyright © Jansen Lim 2024

ISBN 9789815144901

Typeset in Garamond by MAP Systems, Bengaluru, India

www.penguin.sg

*For my mother, who has regaled me with
many colourful stories of her past, birthing
the anatomy of this book*

Part I

Chapter One

From her vantage point, Lorong Limau stood alone; all of its single-storey shacks, whether they were fronted by clothes hanging on bamboo poles or marred by a fading coat of paint, were gathered in unison. Standing atop a knoll about five hundred metres away, Tin accorded herself a sweeping panorama of her village—rooftops cascading in mottled shades of red, the surrounding large trees partially blocking some shacks from view, thereby rendering the entire setting an aura of mystery, air wells punctuating the facade in a zigzag pattern almost like dots of grey bouncing off a gigantic palette. As far as she was concerned, the view was worthy of admiration and had never failed to soothe her nerves in times of anxiety. Like this very morning when she woke up and started fretting about the secret endeavour that she would be carrying out after running an errand in the market. She told no one about it, not even Molly, her closest friend who also happened to be her next-door neighbour. It was simply something she had to do despite feeling uneasy about how it might eventually affect her.

Earlier, an encounter with her sister, Gau Pee, before she could even step out of the house only served to fray at the seams of her anxiety.

'Why are you going out this early?' Gau Pee questioned her. As usual, her sister spoke as if she were commanding a firing squad. Even the look on her face, nostrils tightening, eyes narrowing, befitted one who gave the final order of execution.

'Shhh, let's not wake everyone up,' Tin responded, 'I have my reasons.' Her composure belied the nerves surrounding her real intent.

Not easily hoodwinked, Gau Pee probed further. 'What reason? You usually leave for the market much later, which means you're probably doing something behind my back that you're not telling me.' Her voice was not as loud this time around but still no less forceful. 'Does your best friend have anything to do with this? I know she's always up to no good!' By best friend she, of course, meant Molly for whom she held nothing but utter contempt.

Boxed in by concrete walls and cement flooring, the living room where both sisters stood was sparse in furniture, save a round wooden table with six chairs of the same cheap-looking build and a rather rickety cupboard made of plywood and plastic. It was dark and fuggy, and since everyone else had not woken up yet, an eerie air of quiet prevailed.

Gau Pee was still in her pyjamas. Tin was wearing, as usual, a threadbare *samfu*—Chinese garb comprising a short-sleeve blouse with a pair of matching pants, which made her look even tattier given its dull pastel blue colour, obviously a hand-me-down from one of her older sisters. But, in spite of her dressing, people in her village and beyond would often want to catch a second glimpse of her trim, tomboyish figure and the curls of her shoulder-length hair, bouncing in sync with her gait. Unlike Molly, Tin was not blatantly pretty but she was no less a subject of rubbernecking.

'No, this has nothing to do with Molly.'

'Then what?'

'Okay, the truth is I'm planning to go to Hokkien Street to look for a doctor who comes highly recommended by some aunties I spoke with at the market yesterday. They said he might be able to help Ma.' Tin remained calm, concocting a lie on the fly that would hopefully grind her sister's curiosity to a halt once and for all.

At the mention of their mother, Gau Pee seemed placated and said not a word more, immediately extricating herself from Tin's path.

It's going to be all right . . . all it'll take is just one look and no one has to know about this, Tin assured herself as she prepared to make her way to the market en route to her final destination. Here she was on the knoll, transfixed by the scene before her, taking a couple of deep breaths as though trying to assimilate the entire sweep of the morning—a bird's-eye view of the shacks, the thick, dewy air, her village slowly rumbling to life, with the men getting ready for work and the women beginning their household chores—into her petite bosom.

Throughout her life thus far, sixteen years and counting, she had mostly adhered to her visceral bearings, doing what would make her feel connected to her authentic self, even if it meant risking the consequences of her actions. One time, not too long ago, she had secretly gone against her mother's instruction. 'Never teach anyone outside this family to make tarts and cookies so that we'll have less competition in the marketplace to contend with,' Tin's mother had repeatedly emphasized to her children. Despite this, Tin had imparted some baking skills to Molly so that the latter might have another avenue to make more money for her family that had been going through a rough financial patch.

Tin's mother had subsequently found out about her daughter's 'betrayal' from a random conversation she'd had with Molly's mum. She had caned Tin with every ounce of her being, forcing her to ensure Molly's tarts would never see the light of day, or she would face the prospect of more caning. On the heels of her mother's outburst, Tin had mostly stayed home to allow the bloody lashes on her arms and legs to heal so as not to give people a chance to stare awkwardly at her in public. She had also recounted her misadventure to Molly who had obviously felt terribly sorry for her friend and agreed without hesitation to stop making any more tarts and cookies for sale.

The soft, dreamy sun had since taken possession of every corner of Lorong Limau, with its dents and alcoves catching light much like the hidden grudges manifesting in unexpected ways among its inhabitants. Needless to say, grudges were as de rigueur as secrets and gossip in a village like this where people were living in close quarters and would often take the trouble to find out what was happening in the lives of their neighbours, down to the number of unmended holes in their undergarments. Also, the villagers were mostly large families with at least eight to twelve children in each household. In the 1950s, a large proportion of married couples in Singapore were as fertile as the wild bunnies roaming free in the fields. Despite drought, flood, war, you name it, it was hard to find a man with his instrument hanging juiceless between his legs at any time.

'The more kids you have, the rosier your prospects,' Tin's father would frequently proclaim to his children while grabbing his wiener rather unabashedly through his trousers, much to the embarrassment of his wife, who would often shake her head in mock disgust and look away from him. He was banking on the promise of a financially comfortable future, given that more children would probably lead to more earning power in the years to come.

At forty years old, Tin's father was tall and sinewy and had a slight hunch, his skin reminded one of used sandpaper and his voice resembled the sound of a rusty door hinge. He was also vituperative and temperamental, *gan-ni-na* (which meant 'fuck' in Hokkien dialect) being his favourite cuss word. On days when he did not have to go to his office, a small logistics firm where he worked as a clerk, typing and filing documents on a freelance schedule matching that of commodities such as unprocessed rubber and plastic imported into the country, he would potter around the house in his white undershirt and a pair of wrinkled khaki shorts and would never stop barking gan-ni-na. He would curse at a flimsy rug that almost made him slip and fall, swear at his wife for not adding enough vinegar to the pickles, rail against the rats that infiltrated the kitchen, and shout at himself for accidentally bumping his toe against a cupboard or table while making his way from one part of the house to another.

'Gan-ni-na, if you ever abandon your parents and do not bother to support them financially when they grow old,' you will face a prolonged unspeakable kind of suffering,' he would often remind his children sternly, after delivering his more-kids-rosier-prospects maxim. At the sound of his expletive, Tin and her siblings would shudder and vow in silence to remain devoted to their parents for as long as they lived; taking a cue from their father, they would also each keep a mental note to have plenty of children of their own in the future, God willing, regardless of whether they could ultimately emerge from the throes of poverty.

In fact, many living in Tin's neighbourhood were extremely poor, surviving from one pay cheque to another yet seldom allowing poverty to hamstring their appetite for procreation. A running joke among the villagers was that you can easily spot more pregnant women hanging around in Lorong Limau than the aggregate number of chickens kept in all of their backyards. Of course, it might be unfair to draw this analogy because only the slightly more well-to-do, few and far between, could afford to rear chickens for consumption. The rest of the throng would mostly subsist on vegetables, like bean sprouts, tapioca, and kale, and would only get the chance to consume chicken once a year during their respective new year celebrations. Still, it's hard not to notice the number of baby bumps popping up every other week or month in the village.

You may then ask yourself why these villagers seemed to produce more and more children when they could not even fill the stomachs of their existing ones. The answer would be multifold: birth control measures were non-existent at that time; it was normal if not expected for a fertile married woman not only to experience two pregnancies in the stretch of a year, for example, one in January and another in December, but to stay productive till her late forties; self-administered abortion through the consumption of an inordinate quantity of wild pineapple, saffron, or other causal herbs was highly unpredictable in terms of the end result, and in some cases life-threatening, so many women tended to avoid it; if the couple truly could not afford to raise the child, they would give it up for adoption in exchange for a nominal fee that would cover the cost of hiring a midwife to deliver the baby as well as the cost of preparing special food that would help the birth mother regain her strength in the shortest time possible—stir-fried chicken in sesame sauce with either glutinous rice wine or brandy for the wealthy; pig intestines and kidneys boiled in soup with black pepper for the poor.

Incidentally, Tin's mother gave up her baby daughter for adoption shortly after childbirth just a few days ago. It was the fourth child in their family history that 'had to be sent away', a phrase that had made its way into the parlance of Tin's parents. Nine months earlier, after Tin's mother had discovered that she was pregnant with this child, Tin's father wasted no time in kick-starting negotiations with childless couples as well as wealthy ones already with children of their own—some of whom were distant relatives, others recommended by common friends—to see if any of these parties would be interested and committed enough to bring up the child as their own. He knew that he simply could not afford to have yet another addition to his thriving bunch of six: Pao (oldest daughter, twenty years of age, married to a middle-class gentleman from a neighbouring village with a six-month-old son, which in turn qualified Tin's mother as one of the esteemed members of the Pregnant Grandmothers Club in Lorong Limau), Gau Pee (second daughter, nineteen years old, maritally toxic), Ah Hock (the first son, eighteen years old, an apple that did not fall too far from the tree, as temperamental as his father), Tin (third daughter, sixteen years old, the family's black sheep), Bok Koon (second son, fifteen years old, book-smart) and Kee Kee (youngest daughter, thirteen years old, nicknamed 'the princess').

After meeting up with Tin's parents a number of times, one childless couple, the husband a watchmaker and the wife a homemaker, had agreed to adopt the baby provided it carried no major physical defect such as the loss of a limb, blindness, or missing toes. They also agreed to reimburse Tin's parents with slightly more money if it were a boy, since boys were generally favoured over girls by many Singaporean Chinese people for the simple reason that males were likely to propagate future generations, thus keeping the family surname intact unlike girls who would one day get married and then go on to assume their husband's surname.

At one point in their conversation, after both sides had more or less come to an agreement, the watchmaker's wife asked Tin's mother, 'I'm not sure how to say this but uh . . . would you want to maybe spend a few days with your child after delivery? I mean it'll be fine with me, you know. I totally get it.' Her voice was as delicate as the construct of her face, which looked as if it were about to splinter into bits in the wake of an earthquake. Caution was also duly executed as she uttered '*your* child' instead of '*the* child' or worse, '*my* child', not wanting to give the wrong impression that she was already stripping Tin's mother of her maternal entitlement even before the child had been born.

'That won't be necessary. You can have the baby once it's born,' Tin's mother had replied succinctly. Thirty-six years of age, blessed with a smooth complexion and sharp facial features, she appeared distant, wearing a perpetual expression of heartlessness, determined to let the child be whisked away without any hint of regret or guilt. Her hair was gathered into a bun, her arms were spindly, and she somehow managed to maintain a slender figure despite getting pregnant repeatedly after marriage. Throughout the past couple of meetings with these adoptive parents, Tin's mother rarely uttered anything beyond what was expected of her, leaving it to her husband to manage the negotiations and iron out the details. Most of the time, she would listen and nod in acquiescence with what he was saying, hardly eking out a friendly smile, not even a fake one to assure the couple that the child in her womb, the one they would be inheriting, might turn out to be as warm and friendly as its biological mother.

Judging from her impassiveness, one would likely attribute her current stupor after parturition less to the emotional toll of giving up her fourth child in a row for adoption and more to the physical toll of carrying a baby to full term one pregnancy after another. Tin's mother had gotten married at the tender age of fifteen, had her first child the year after, and subsequently had seventeen more, eight of which ended up stillborn. Although one thing was for sure, her health was fast deteriorating and if she did not replenish her body with the necessary nutrients, she would only get weaker by the day and might suffer the same fate as that of her relatives, all in their mid-thirties and mired in a pregnancy merry-go-round, who had resisted spending whatever measly sum of money they had in their possession for post-birth recuperation and had their lives cut short.

To prevent the same misfortune from befalling her mother, Tin had to make a trip to the market this morning, her secret agenda notwithstanding, to buy some pig intestines as per the instruction given by Gau Pee, her authoritative older sister who had confronted her earlier, before she could even step out of the house. Gau Pee was incidentally her mum's favourite child, whom she likened to a modern-day witch given that her nose was as aquiline as that of a fabled sorceress she had chanced upon in an old picture storybook owned by Molly.

Following her visit to the market, she would carry out her secret mission and hopefully make it back home within a reasonable timeframe lest she might arouse suspicion in Gau Pee who would happily inform their father that she had been loitering in the streets for fun—purposely leaving out the bit about Tin looking for a doctor at Hokkien Street—instead of returning home on time to tend to their mother's poor health. For that, she would probably end up getting caned by her father, with Gau Pee watching the spectacle and smirking in the background. No, she must not allow that to happen. After a moment's thought, she trundled down the knoll and headed straight to the market.

Meanwhile, Tin's mother had been lying in bed for five days except for the few times she needed to heed her biological calls and to drink coffee, her favourite beverage, which also happened to fill her stomach whenever she was hungry and when there wasn't any food left in the house. She had not been eating well either, a little bit of radish here, some pickles there, reduced to skin and bones in a rather short time, more so given that she had already been thin prior to this episode of being infirm. It goes without saying that she had been unable to manage the cooking and laundry in her household, all of which had since been relegated to Gau Pee, the next matron-in-command, as the oldest daughter Pao was already married and no longer around to hold the reins. Even when Pao moved out, their shack was as crammed as ever—Tin's parents occupied one bedroom, Ah Hock and Bok Koon another, and the three girls, Gau Pee, Tin, and Kee Kee slept on makeshift mattresses in the kitchen, which made more sense than if they were to sleep in the living room since the kitchen was more spacious and had better ventilation with two windows facing the backyard, a vast space of nothing but undulating greenery. At times, Kee Kee would quietly tow her mattress to her parents' bedroom after they were fast asleep, having realized early on that there were less cockroaches crawling in that space compared to the kitchen floor, what with leftover food crumbs and deep cracks in the walls, ripe for the hibernation of cockroaches. But now with her mother coughing rampantly and sighing aloud, Kee Kee decided it would be better to secure a good night's sleep in the kitchen despite cockroaches and ants scuttling around— all three girls had acquired the art of flicking such insects off their skin without breaking their sleep cycle—than experience an unending staccato of illness-triggered noises in her parents' room.

It remained somewhat puzzling, though, to all in Tin's family how their mother had given over to her current condition, hardly a word uttered, her clothes unchanged since the delivery of the baby, possessing not even a shred of interest in the goings-on among her children. A striking contrast to the past when she seemed to have been able to bounce back into doing housework shortly after every childbirth, as though she had a secret compartment in her body providing her the strength and vitality for the resumption of her day-to-day chores. Now, she was all frail and cooped up in the dark, fuggy bedroom, lit only by one candle that threw a dance of shadows across the cracked grey stucco on the wall. *Could she be distressed over giving up her child for adoption?* they questioned. But then it would not have been the first time. The last three pregnancies saw her doing the same with striking equanimity. If she'd had any regret parting with each of those three daughters, she certainly showed no sign of it. Even during the times when her pregnancies resulted in stillborn babies, when things looked their bleakest, she managed to somehow snap back to life after a good cry. But strangely, this time around, she showed no hint of reclaiming her energy; in fact, she was uncharacteristically aloof, her face ashen with a blend of grief and exhaustion.

Her husband, Tin's father, had also been unusually reticent about the whole matter. Normally, he would spout his gan-ni-na at the slightest inertia demonstrated by his wife, like the one time she was late at preparing dinner due to a sprained ankle ('Gan-ni-na, don't tell me you're slow because you have to cook with your legs?') or whenever she hesitated before agreeing with whatever decision he had made on behalf of the family ('Gan-ni-na, what took you so long to agree with me?'). With his wife bedridden over the past few days, he simply let her be, hoping she would eventually recover and assume her workhorse persona after consuming the pig intestine soup that Gau Pee planned to brew with the necessary ingredients upon Tin's return from the market, something they would not have been able to afford were it not for the stipulated sum of money given by the adoptive parents. Still, there were a few instances when he felt a blind compulsion to storm into their bedroom—he'd since vacated his territory, half the bed to be precise, by sleeping on a mattress in the boys' room so that she could have some quiet time to heal—to bark at his wife for not mending the hole in one of his socks or getting rid of a persistent stain on his trousers, to crush her listless thin body under his lean yet agile musculature, to vilify her, to pull her hair out. In his imagination, he would kick her out of bed and make her realize that her behaviour was simply intolerable yet he continued to hold his tongue and rein in his impulses. Self-restraint aside, he knew what had been troubling her more than he was willing to let on.

'Would you like me to massage your legs, maybe fetch you another cup of coffee or bring you some biscuits?' Her daughters Gau Pee and Tin would sometimes stop by at her room and ask in the midst of doing housework, their voices instinctively reduced to a whisper the moment they opened their mouths and talked to her. Lying in bed and gazing vacantly at practically nothing, she would then slowly roll over and turn her back to them, her body looking as fragile as a heap of cotton wool. They would regard her gesture as a faint protest, a cue for them to leave her alone. In the end, any attempt on their part to help her get back on her feet continued to reverberate empty. Sometimes she could be seen dozing off with her mouth slightly open or pretending to be (no one could be certain), wheezing a little, her slender frame perched on its right side, which happened to be her preferred sleeping position, her fingers slightly stirring as though endowed with a secret life of their own. Sometimes, in the thick of the night, she could be heard expectorating repeatedly until her sputum was freed from her lungs.

Of course, in the time to come, she would heal or least appear to have gotten better as the long-suffering women of her generation tended to hide their pain behind stoic facades. She would allow some sense of urgency to pierce through her languor and prevent her from falling deeper into her rabbit hole of self-affliction; she would wake up one day and look at whatever had been troubling her from a deliberate remove and resume her matriarchal obligations, such as keeping the household together and attending to the needs of her husband and children. Her time spent helplessly stuck in bed would be over as quickly as it had unexpectedly emerged. Of course, her family would attribute her recovery to the pig intestine soup. After all, it had proven to be a remedy time and again for women in a similar situation although in the case of Tin's mother it could not have been further from the truth. All the pig intestines in the world could not save her from herself if she continued to resist convalescence.

She was utterly heartbroken, that was the intractable truth. She had wanted to keep this daughter so badly that nothing else mattered, not her health, not even her sanity.

Down on her druthers, Tin's mother had practically been reduced to the equivalent of a sleepwalker. That she had more or less steeled herself against an emotional collapse or any physical dilapidation in the three earlier cases where she had given up her daughters for adoption owed itself to one glaring factor: all three were born in the broken month of the Chinese calendar, wherein each zodiac sign would be tagged with one broken month per lunar year. For instance, a child born under the sign of dragon in the twelfth month would be considered broken, cow in the third, goat in the ninth, and so forth. According to Chinese belief, girls born in the broken month were generally recognized as toxic, highly unlikely to get married and even if they did, they would bring bad luck, shame, loss of wealth, and possibly death to their husbands and offspring. However, this was not the case with the present child.

During each of those three pregnancies, Tin's mother had already had a good guesstimate—women in that era never really knew when they started conceiving and could only make a rough assessment based on the weight of their womb—that her child would be born in the broken month. So, it was ultimately a relatively less arduous task getting over her grief after childbirth, repeatedly consoling herself that daughters born in the broken month were taboo, no matter her maternal possessiveness. It would be a gross exaggeration, however, to say that she'd had no qualms giving up her daughters to be raised by other people. Naturally, like most mothers, she was struck with unadulterated guilt. But each time she felt conflicted, she would take deep breaths and exhale slowly, insisting her daughters would be better off elsewhere than having to miss out on the goodness of life due to their poverty so long as the adoptive parents, all of whom were unable to produce a child of their own, did not mind having girls born in the broken month.

Conversely, if the newborn were a son, she and Tin's father might have tried their utmost best to raise him— borrowing money from relatives, finding more part-time jobs—since boys born in the broken month were regarded less harshly albeit far from ideal. Needless to say, many if not all adoption negotiations would also include the prerogative of the biological parents to revoke the deal should the child turn out to be a son instead of a daughter born in the aforementioned month because it's believed that the son's disadvantageous situation can be mollified through prayers and may even be eradicated with adequate spiritual guidance.

But this pregnancy of hers had been different. Her guesstimate suggested that her child might not be born in the broken month.

'I have to keep this baby even if it's a girl,' she had told her husband late one night when their children were already asleep, probably six to seven months into her pregnancy, long after the adoption negotiation was finalized.

'Gan-ni-na, are you crazy? We can't even afford to feed our existing kids and you're telling me you want to keep this new one!' Tin's father protested, eyeing her fiercely.

'Shhh, don't wake them up,' she said, her voice a mere squeak. 'What I'm saying is perhaps we should give this matter another round of thought. I mean I can always make more pastries and cookies to sell, and I can ask around to see if anyone, especially the wealthy folks from Riverside village and Kallang Park, would want to engage my sewing services. Please, I beg of you, let's not give up this baby. This one's not going to be born in the broken month.'

'No way!' he asserted, though less loudly than earlier.

'What if it's a boy? I'm sure you would want to keep him,' she implored.

'We simply don't have the money and besides, your home-made pastries and tailoring services are not going to change our predicament much, so there's no way we're going to keep this child, boy or girl, and that's final. I'm going to bed,' he said, leaving her heavy-headed and bleary-eyed.

Chapter Two

'Would you have any idea where Kallang Gardens is?' Tin asked Molly out of the blue one breezy evening, just a couple of days before she went about executing her secret mission. Both girls were lying down on a large rattan mat that they had spread out on a field located diagonally across from their shacks. It was the end-of-the-day ritual they had been carrying out since their childhood days. Mostly, they would talk about the happenings of the day itself while enjoying the cool air after the sun had set. At times, their tête-à-tête would be accompanied by a little snacking on the side if either party was fortunate enough to have leftover bread for the day to be shared with each other. Some days there just was not much to be said, each in her own abyss, held safe and tight by the other's silence. No forced camaraderie, no awkward communion, just the savouring of each other's company and some delightful stargazing if the stars were out gallivanting in the nightscape, which happened to be the case that evening.

'Ooh, isn't Kallang Gardens rather far from here?' Molly answered, looking skyward.

'How far?'

The eventide stretched out before them in a wide, empty expanse. The sky was darkening, and the stars gleamed. The day's shadows were pulled back from the distance, gathering at the foot of their houses. In the fifties, outdoor spaces in Singapore such as roads and fields were mostly unlit at night; neither lamp posts nor any form of street lights existed during that time. As a result, Singaporeans then were used to walking and peddling their bicycles in the dark if they were out and about—not that there was a bevy of night activities they could partake in with the exception of *wayang*s, staged performances that took place once or twice a year, and the goings-on at the renowned New World Entertainment, a pay-per-entry, one-stop venue for games, music, and food. Many would rather stay put in the vicinity of their respective villages instead of venturing out at night, usually laying out a mat on some nearby field after dinner and chatting with neighbours till they ran out of things to say and eventually retreating to their own homes for hopefully a good night's sleep.

Given the non-existence of proper outdoor lighting, you may easily draw the conclusion that snatch theft must have been a rampant consequence for those who walked or cycled in pitch darkness, but the reality was that it was as uncommon as finding someone with long-sightedness threading needles just for the fun of it. It simply would not make any financial sense for one poor person to rob another of his ilk. Thieves would be better off working their stuff in more well-to-do neighbourhoods like Kallang Gardens and Selegie where Chinese landlords and Jews congregated respectively but even so, cases were known to be far and few between. Robbery aside, even molestation and rape were anomalies, hard as it may be for any Singaporean living in present times to imagine.

'Why are you asking about Kallang Gardens?' Molly inquired, still gazing at the stars, her chirpy voice momentarily drowning out the chirps of nearby crickets.

'No reason really,' Tin muttered, her head gently propped up from behind by her interlocked hands, and, like Molly, her gaze directed at the sky.

Quiet prevailed thereafter. Wild bunnies that would normally run riot on the field in the day were nowhere to be seen, probably hiding in their enclaves from any potential disturbance or danger. A legion of fireflies had emerged from nowhere to puncture the breath of nightfall with skittish incandescence. Milling and undulating in a single swarm, they stretched so high and dense that they momentarily obscured the darkness. Both girls sat up and soaked in the beautiful, giddy display of lights, agape and speechless, although Tin could have sworn she did hear Molly mumble a near-silent 'wow'. After the fireflies had drifted far afield, they lay down once again with their back on the mat, thinking to themselves how little they needed to set their hearts racing.

'Do you think one day I'll be forced into marrying someone I don't fancy?' Molly murmured, breaking the silence between them that was as natural and comfortable as their ritualistic, verbose exchange. 'Well, you know, girls like us. We'll probably have to go through matchmaking and end up with the ugliest fart ever as a husband!'

'You? I don't think so. You're too smart for that,' Tin said with a giggle.

'Hmm.'

Again, a brief round of silence descended on their chit-chat. Still with her eyes locked at the starry canvas, Molly imagined what her future husband would look like and how it would feel to have sex with him the first time. Of the same age as Gau Pee, she'd thought about sex quite a bit since her menstruation and had a vague idea of what an orgasm amounted to.

'I'll find out the location of Kallang Gardens, like how far it is from here and how to get there by bus. I know this boy who delivers the papers every morning and he seems to know just about every place and happening in Singapore.' Molly offered to help without even asking Tin why Kallang Gardens had seized her interest all of a sudden even though she knew there was more to her inquiry that she was prepared to let on.

Lorong Limau would undoubtedly be abuzz with confabulations each time someone in the village went into labour and disappeared from sight for several days. Unlike present times, women from that era were expected to bounce back to their normal routines a day or two after childbirth. The notion of an extended confinement was unheard of. Thus, if a woman suddenly goes missing after giving birth, you can be sure speculations surrounding her disappearance would rage through the village till she would reappear in public; otherwise the talk would only burgeon into a groundswell of worst-case scenarios on par with the legendary travails of World War II, which racked the lives of many less than a decade ago and etched itself in shades of acrimony on the faces of those whose loved ones were brutally executed by the Japanese during the war.

As expected, no exception was to be made in the case of Tin's mother. When she failed to show up in public on the second day after childbirth, people started talking. A handful of villagers appeared to be genuinely concerned: 'Oh dear, she may not be well given her age and all that wear and tear of pregnancies past.' There were those who seemed unable to resist overstating every risk associated with childbirth: 'I've heard the probability of the baby's legs rather than the head emerging from the mother's body would be much higher for women like her who have gone through countless deliveries . . . sigh . . . I'm afraid to say that no mother or child has ever survived in all these cases.' Some took the opportunity to highlight their grudges, more often than not exaggerating the magnitude of the injustice that they claimed they'd suffered as a result of the person being talked about: 'She deserves whatever punishment God has dealt her for sleeping with my husband . . . sure, I may not have any concrete proof but deep down inside I know for sure.' Others were openly malevolent for no appropriate reason: 'Maybe it's better for her to die anyway.' Most of the time, they could be seen gathering outside Tin's house and chatting away, each trying to outdo the other in terms of sensationalizing the rumour mill. And in every case, they were all women.

'Gan-ni-na, don't you bitches have anything better to do than to gossip about my wife?' Above the hubbub that filled the air outside his shack rose the voice of Tin's father, projecting squarely at the culprits from his window and never failing to make them scurry like mice being chased by a ferocious cat. On one occasion, without even bothering to make out the thread of their conversation—he didn't want to anyway—Tin's father, beside himself with rage at the constant chatter within his earshot, seized a boiling kettle, removed its lid and splashed the hot water at the blabbermouths through the window, scalding one woman's arm and causing the rest to run for the hills.

On the flip side, there would be neighbours who truly cared, like Molly's mother who had been religiously preparing food for Tin's family since the birth of the child, fully aware that Tin's mother would not be well enough to cook for her family shortly after delivery but somewhat taken by surprise later on that she was still bedridden after several days based on what Tin shared with Molly regarding her mother's condition.

Whatever portion of food Molly's mother offered to Tin's family was, in fact, painstakingly carved out of her own pot, since her family, like Tin's, was downright poor. Despite having to share their food with another family, which meant they would be consuming a much smaller portion than their already scrimpy helping on normal days, no one from Molly's family took umbrage at their mother's kindness. Molly's father, a deckhand, was only home once every few months and barely made enough money to support himself let alone his wife and seven children. So, Molly's mother had no choice but to eke out a living by weaving rattan baskets for sale—hence those calloused fingers of hers—and by sewing clothes for the military as well as for wealthy households similar to the mode of operation adopted by Tin's mother who further supported her livelihood by making cookies and pastries.

'Here's some cabbage soup for your family,' said Molly's mother, handing over a pot to Gau Pee at the latter's doorstep. 'Be careful, it's hot.'

'Oh aunty, you're ever so kind. I really hope I can repay you in this lifetime,' exclaimed Gau Pee when she took the pot from Molly's mother.

'Please don't say that . . . we're neighbours after all,' Molly's mother replied with a look of weary compassion. Two years older than Tin's mother, she had been awfully attractive in her younger days with many boys in the village swooning over her. But, sadly, a life fraught with poverty and hardship sure has a way of catching up, and she had since yielded to the inevitability of age in double-quick time. Now, she looked like a dispirited old woman with a stoop shaving two to three inches off her original height.

'I'll cook something different tomorrow, hopefully,' she added, obviously thinking about what other food items she could possibly afford given her impecuniosity.

'Oh aunty, don't you worry. We *love* all the food that you've prepared for us even if it's something that's cooked in your sleep. We are so, so grateful,' Gau Pee exclaimed yet again, this time beaming from ear to ear. To the perceptive, a trait that obviously eluded Molly's mother, Gau Pee's utterance of 'love' appeared to be italicized by sarcasm, underlined by scorn. Moreover, it was hard not to have caught a hint of mockery in her eyes.

It did not take long for Gau Pee to empty the soup into the main drainage that coursed through the back of her house and discard the cabbages into the trash bin after the departure of Molly's mother. She then washed the pot, all prepared to return it to Molly's mother later the same evening and all ready to pay her the highest of compliments for her culinary skills and mostly for her kindness. Throughout the past few days, she'd been enacting the same protocol: gushing over the food when Molly's mother was at her doorstep, trashing it when no one else was watching and then returning the pot or plate or whatever was handed to her to Molly's mother accompanied by words of gratitude and a teary appreciation. 'We're so lucky to have you in our lives, you will always be my second mum.' Well, you get the drift. Who could have guessed she was merely polishing a vindictive streak?

'Stupid mother of a bitch!' Gau Pee mumbled while wiping the pot dry with a dirty rag that she would normally use for clearing cobwebs and dust off the wall. Envisioning how Molly's family would be eating out of this bacteria-laden pot, she flashed a smile that enkindled her bitterest cup of tea: *revenge is the air that I breathe and success smiles on those who know how to manipulate others.*

Since the beginning, Gau Pee had resented Molly— and by association, Molly's mother and everyone else in her family although in their case it was not blatant—simply because Molly was regarded to be as capable and resourceful as she was. For a while, Molly was making pastries with the help of Tin who was subsequently beaten by her mother for divulging the recipe. Whenever she was praised by some villagers for being this or that, Molly's name would invariably weave into the fold. 'You make such delicious *nonya kuehs*, they're just as good as Molly's'; 'I think you and Molly are the best seamstresses of your generation'; 'You're as admirable as Molly for being able to contribute financially to your family at such a tender age.' She hated the sound of *that* name and most of all she hated the person to whom she was often compared.

If there were any justice at all, this bitch should die young so I don't have to ever see her face again and if I were to die earlier, God forbid, I will bequeath my intelligence to her, since she has none—something Gau Pee would often tell herself and then laugh aloud.

Coincidentally, both these nineteen-year-old girls would also find themselves sharing the same taste in boys, which more or less put the sharpest sting in their relationship. What made it worse for Gau Pee was that the guys would pick Molly over her ten out of ten times for reasons beyond her own comprehension albeit crystal clear to others looking in from the outside. In the eyes of these people, Molly was down-to-earth, fun-loving, and pretty, with sparkling black eyes and a pair of luscious lips whereas Gau Pee tended to come across as a superficial teenage girl who looked way older than her age and whose most distinct facial feature, her narrow, crooked nose, which made her look predatory in nature, turned out to be her least appealing trademark. As if that was not lacerating enough, the bane of her life happened to live next door to her, no thanks to some crude kismet connection she would say, and also happened to be best of friends with her sister Tin of all people, so by default she hated Tin just as much if not more for being what she considered a turncoat.

If there's one thing at which Gau Pee was more skilled than Molly could ever imagine for herself, it was her ability to hide her true feelings—hatred, anger, schadenfreude—under a layer of sycophancy. Yet, she also revealed what she only wanted to appear to hide. For sure, her siblings knew better than to upset her for she could remember everything down to the most intricate development of every grudge harboured, including every insult that had been darted in her direction way back from childhood days. She was also perfectly adept at keeping a mental record of every strength and weakness shown by people whom she disliked, every lie or confession uttered by these supposed foes. The apposite point was that there was no finer example of a begrudger than Gau Pee's side of Poseidon—a mythological Greek God famous for bearing grudges for eons—who would constantly seek to exploit her adversaries to her own advantage.

She was in high spirits after getting rid of the cabbage soup from Molly's mum, so much so that she started to dance around the kitchen, humming the tune of 'Bengawan Solo' as she gently swayed her hips. Her exuberance seemed to change its texture every few seconds, one moment over-the-top, another moment self-serving, like the dark surface of the kitchen wall catching the light at different times of the day. However, no sooner did the thought of Tin seep into her mind than her joy short-circuited.

It's been more than two hours since she left for the market. What's taking her such a bloody long time to come back? Gau Pee wondered. *Once that idiot is back, I'll make sure she chops all the wood that's needed to start the fire for my cooking.* For the rest of the morning, she cleaned up the house and prepared lunch with whatever ingredients were available in the kitchen, slicing carrots and leafy vegetables and putting them in a plate, ready to be stir-fried upon Tin's return when she would also start boiling the pig intestine soup for her mother.

The house was relatively empty. She was done with her tasks in the kitchen. Her father was out at work; so was her brother Ah Hock whose job required him to sort letters at the post office; Tin was at the market; their mother was recuperating in bed; Bok Koon, the other brother, had left for school. Gau Pee had always enjoyed the quiet, like this morning, when she could use the uninterrupted peace to contemplate evil thoughts, plotting her next move against Molly and her other foes. Was there more to her life apart from doing housework, scheming against others, and making tarts and cookies for sale? Sadly, no. Did she ever dream of going to school? The answer would be obvious, given her over-achiever inclination. However, during that era, only boys were allowed to have a formal education; girls on the other hand were strictly relegated to housework and part-time jobs. Of course, if they came from a rich family and their parents truly believed in gender equality, cases of which were rather rare, they might just be able to acquire knowledge of English, Mathematics and Science through the services of specially engaged private tutors. All in all, many believed academia was simply pointless for girls.

It was already ten o'clock. Kee Kee, her youngest sister, was still fast asleep much to her annoyance. She approached the mattress on which she was sleeping, gave it a nudge with her foot and said, 'Get up!'

'Gosh, it's still early, isn't it?' Kee Kee strained to speak, feeling drowsy and thirsty at the same time. 'I need my beauty sleep.'

'What you need right now is a kick in your butt!' Gau Pee said in a half-joking manner. Unlike Tin, who was hard-working and responsible, Kee Kee had never lifted a finger to share the burden of housework—laundry, cooking, cleaning of the floor—with Gau Pee. So, in that sense, she certainly lived up to her moniker 'the princess', reminding everyone from time to time that she had been dealt the cruellest hand that life could deal: a damsel, elegant and refined by nature, born into a family of indigent background. And, unlike Tin, she was firmly in Gau Pee's good books because she had always made it a point to agree with her older sister on whatever matters and during scenarios of conflict. And it helped that she was always saying nasty things about Molly even though in reality she had nothing against the latter.

'Please, Gau Pee, I'm not feeling well this morning,' she moaned. Only a dodo would not be able to recognize this as one of her many fibs to tear herself away from performing household chores. Excuses like 'Oh I can't go to the market, my foot is hurting so badly' and 'I'm not comfortable holding a knife' and 'I'm too scared to go near a fire' were heard all too frequently whenever she was pressed to contribute to the running of their household. Even with Tin's mother shouting at her and on a few occasions caning her till she bled, she still would not give in. After a while, everyone became so sick of trying to get her to do her part that she was mostly left alone to spend her days beautifying her hair with flowers, which she would pluck from nearby fields, and fantasizing about having tea with her idols, namely, William Holden and Vivien Leigh.

'Okay, you can sleep a bit more but promise me you'll help me this afternoon to carry out you-know-what,' Gau Pee said with a malicious wink and smile. They had planned to slip a few dead cockroaches into one of the pockets on Molly's samfu, which used to be washed and hung daily on the clothesline—it was easy to spot Molly's clothes, as she owned only two pairs of samfu, one bright red, one off-brown—and hopefully get a good laugh out of watching her reaction from behind their front door when the time came for her to retrieve her family's clothes in the late afternoon, usually dried and crisp by then.

'Oh . . . I get it,' Kee Kee replied, breaking into a zippy laugh that obviously ran counter to her lack of energy displayed just a few seconds ago when she claimed she was not feeling well. As soon as her older sister was out of the scene, she fell back into a deep sleep, slobbering away as time marched on.

Gau Pee then proceeded to check on their mother to see if she needed anything, at the same time maybe gently persuading her to have a bit of breakfast, for she had been sustaining only on coffee and biscuits and skipping the main meals altogether. Incidentally, this was one of Gau Pee's rare displays of compassion. For what it was worth, adjectives like 'kind' and 'empathetic' tended to lose their meaning in the eyes of someone like her unless the person in need of kindness and empathy happened to be her mother with whom she had always been awfully close. Only her mum, not even her father. She would act respectfully towards the latter out of fear and not because she had any compassion for him. As for everyone else, they should consider themselves lucky if they had only been at the receiving end of her casual taunts and not something more sinister, which would break their spirit once and for all.

The moment she entered her mother's room, she was reduced to speechlessness before mustering a shriek that could potentially shatter the hardiest of glasses. The bed was empty. Her mum was nowhere to be found.

Chapter Three

By this time, Tin was already at the open-air market, the one and only place from where she obtained fresh produce on a daily basis. There were of course several other similar markets dotting the landscape of Singapore but this one was at the heart of Lorong Limau. As usual, the market was noisy and crowded and every vendor was out peddling his goods full throttle, some of which were displayed in propped-up carts while others were placed on tarpaulins spread out on the ground. It would be easy to drift from stall to stall until they all blur into a muddled mass if you were to ask someone who has never done any marketing in her life to describe the experience. However, certain stalls, like those selling livestock, namely chickens and ducks, would differentiate themselves better from the others for one reason: the transaction itself would be a visually gruesome spectacle especially for the faint of heart. Whenever customers made a purchase, the fowls would be retrieved from their cages, sliced at the throat, drained of blood, then defeathered almost immediately, soaked in boiling water and subsequently eviscerated. First-time buyers would usually gasp in horror; even seasoned witnesses like Tin would often scurry past these stalls, unwilling to stomach what many reckoned to be one of the most casually savage acts committed by mankind in public, yet few would be terrified to the point of abstaining from eating chickens or ducks for the rest of their lives.

'Yuks,' Tin muttered upon catching a glimpse of the barbarity.

Without delay, she headed straight to the stall selling pork and offal, a vendor from whom her family had been buying meat for years. They called her Ah Pui, meaning 'fat' in Hokkien dialect. The bedraggled woman—firmly on the obese side, sporting a jade pendant necklace and a jade ring on one of her fingers to match, her frowsy oversized samfu billowing about her—butchered pigs with both the heft of a locomotive train and the dexterity of a card sharp. Unlike her fellow vendors selling chickens and ducks, Ah Pui did not have to subject buyers to the same code of cruelty, as the pigs were already killed and eviscerated before being hauled to the market for sale.

In the past minute or two, she had been busy fiddling with her steelyard balance, a beam with arms of unequal length incorporating a counterweight that would slide along the calibrated longer arm to balance the load in question and render its weight. On one hand, she would gingerly remove a slice of pork from the paper bag attached to the steelyard balance and on another, she would hesitate for a fractional moment and then put back the same slice of pork into the bag only to take it out again in the next instance. It was like watching a film reel on repeat. Ahead of Tin in the queue was a customer haggling with Ah Pui who just could not seem to decide whether to surrender that slice of pork amounting to no less than one gram in weight or to hold it back for sale to the next customer.

'Oh my god, what's your problem?' the irritated customer—a lady in her fifties—took aim at her.

'No problem, lah, I just have to make sure you get exactly what you pay for,' Ah Pui snapped back, still fiddling with the balance.

'For goodness' sake, can't you be generous enough not to quibble over a couple of milligrams? I mean seriously, how much money can you lose if you were to let go of that tiny piece of meat?' the customer rejoined.

'Just a minute,' she said, this time taking a different slice of pork—twice as thick as the first one—out of the bag and determining if the balance was in equilibrium. Indeed, and finally, it was.

'Oh my god, I don't believe this,' the customer muttered, gently slapping her forehead with her hand. 'Can you stop being so calculative? No wonder they say women like you will never ever be blessed with a son because your heart is just as small as the crack of your backside!'

'Choy, choy, choy! Stop cursing me so early in the morning,' Ah Pui said, laughing it off and handing over the paper bag to the customer without a second more of hesitation. Had she contemplated further on her customer's retort, she might have realized there was a whole lot of truth to it: her eleven children were all daughters. After her last pregnancy, she had not been sure if she would be ready to try her luck again, more concerned about the mental well-being of her husband who seemed to have lost faith in the gods after witnessing time and again the absence of a penis on every package that emerged from her womb. From her seventh delivery onwards, he would fall to his knees and bawl like a child in front of her bed, lending the impression that he was shedding tears of joy when in fact it was anything but that. Without fail, she would sob along, and the midwife would congratulate them both saying, 'Oh, it's so rare to see such consistently overjoyed parents.'

Pressed for time, Tin managed to foist her request on Ah Pui: 'Thirty cents of pig intestines,' she spoke loudly after elbowing her way past new patrons to the front of the queue. Ah Pui heeded Tin's request and proceeded to attach a new load to the steelyard balance and, as expected, fiddled with it repeatedly till she was satisfied with the outcome. Tin made her payment, left the market, and crossed the main thoroughfare to the bus depot in order to take a bus to Kallang Gardens, the venue where she was to execute her plan.

It took the better part of a late humid morning and a little reconnaissance to locate the terrace house where her baby sister would henceforth be raised and sequestered in name and spirit from her biological family. Tin had rarely wandered beyond the confines of Lorong Limau, as everything she ever needed—food, medicine, household accessories, or even potential boyfriends—was to be found within a fifteen-minute walking radius of her village. She managed to get to this point—finding the address and ascertaining its location—due, in part, to her deliberate eavesdropping on her parents' conversations with the adoptive couple, and, in part, to Molly's resourcefulness in providing specifics, like direction, bus route, building descriptors as well as vicarious impressions of Kallang Gardens as a village, the Kallang river coursing through it, a spacious thoroughfare, and pockets of shops selling traditional Chinese herbs. For that, she asked Molly to thank the paper boy on her behalf, the source of Molly's detailed research, who happened to be running errands for the wealthy folks in Kallang Gardens and Clarke Quay.

Before embarking on this journey, Tin had wondered how she was going to pull the whole thing off without encountering interlopers, primarily passers-by and neighbours of the adoptive couple. Luckily, it was not a problem worth sweating over as she now realized. Kallang Gardens was a relatively quiet residential neighbourhood with hardly anyone loitering outside its well-maintained, off-white, single-storey terrace houses arranged in rows much like cemetery tombstones, each with its own frontal patch of green and demarcated from another by a narrow cement walkway.

Now all she had to do was steal a glance—just one glance would be enough to make her happy, her way of bidding valediction to a sister she would probably never have the chance to acknowledge in public—through one of the open windows of the house, hopefully without being seen by anyone inside. But first, she was going to search for the right window to take a peek, since she would not know which part of the house her baby sister was in.

Trapped between the pressure of her excitement and the burden of her sentimentality, Tin feared this would be another case of déjà vu, one more in a repeated series of catching covert glimpses of her sisters given up for good to the care of other families, which, in its formulaic anticipation, would merely end up lacerating no one but herself. In the past, she would mope for a few days after each sighting; her mood would generally be sombre, appetite razed, eyes slightly watery each time she recalled their images, all evoking a certain downcast emanation.

She approached the house as a thief would, her footfalls involuntarily muted by the grass. But, in an attempt to peek through the front window of the house, she accidentally crunched her sandals on the gravel. She recoiled in alarm, immediately squatting down beneath the window frame, hoping no one else was alerted by the sound. For a while, nothing seemed to stir. She inhaled and waited, continuing in repeat mode for a minute or two. After that, she stood up slowly and peeked, her head just barely above the lower frame but there was no baby in sight. What she saw instead was merely the living room, spacious, clean, and decked with high-end teak furniture, devoid of any human presence. She then stealthily inched her way to the backyard along the perimeter of the house, half-suspecting she might be able to find more windows there.

True enough, there were three windows. The first one into which she happened to peer led to the kitchen. Again, no baby. But there she was, the adoptive mother, her back facing Tin, stirring some soup or gravy inside a large cauldron over an iron trivet. Slim and petite, she could easily pass off as a teenager if it were not for her bouffant hair that made her look more matronly than she deserved to be. It was not difficult for Tin to read the back of her head like most people could a facial expression: the adoptive mother seemed happy. What was more, nothing could throw the light-heartedness of her mood into relief so convincingly as the sinuous rhythmic gait of hers—gliding from one corner of the kitchen to another to either fetch a bottle of salt or gather some sliced tomatoes to be scattered inside the cauldron. Even the hem of her skirt was swaying in metronomic sync with her body's rhythm. Indeed, she was happy.

The essence of happy to Tin had long acquired the habit of growing sterile and banal in the abstract—considering her pointedly different living conditions and how often she had to endure swipes from Gau Pee—until this very moment when she glimpsed the moving image of her sister's adoptive mother in her lovely sundress jauntily cooking away in her equally lovely kitchen. *That's being happy, I guess . . . Is this how rich people feel most of the time? Will they be able to recognize themselves in the experience of the poor and make their suffering and pain matter to them as much as their own with a mere thimbleful of empathy? Will they truly understand what it means to live in a miasma of constant financial apocalypse?* For the most part, she had yet to befriend anyone wealthy so it would not be fair for her to make a judgement. Every person she knew in Lorong Limau was unequivocally if not downright poor.

Tin ducked her head just in time to hunker down the moment the adoptive mother turned around and started walking towards the window. *Oh gosh, she must have seen me.* But she had not. What she did see was a tuft of her own hair on the floor, which she duly picked up and discarded through the window. It descended, of all places, on the strip of skin between Tin's nose and her upper lip. Aghast, she wiped it off with the back of her hand. Still in her crouching position, Tin waited for a while before moving to the next window. Conscious of how dry her mouth felt after all that brisk walking and sprinting earlier, feeling the heat and dust at the back of her throat, she longed to gulp down a tall glass of water. *Yes, that's the first thing I'll do when I get home.*

Stealing a glimpse from the second window, she was greeted this time by a bedroom, obviously the couple's. A wooden platform bed occupied the centre of the area, a dressing table on the left and an armoire on the right, all elegantly arranged to arouse a warm fuzzy feeling. A sizeable part of the floor was carpeted with what appeared to be a rather expensive oriental rug, probably imported from overseas, and the walls were dressed up in a coat of shimmering blue paint. And at the foot of the bed, her baby sister—presumably, since the couple had been childless all along before the adoption based on what Tin had gathered from their conversations with her parents—could be seen napping quietly in a cot. Her hair was wavy yet brittle, her left cheek cross-hatched with a lattice of red lines, possibly from sleeping on that side of her face, with her skin dented against the fabric of the towel on which she had been resting, and her body frame a tad on the chubby side.

Not for one moment did she take her eyes off her baby sister. If she could, she would have jumped through the window and wrapped her in a tight squeeze. Underneath the flood of monosyllables—'oh', 'wow', 'hmmm'—there bubbled up an inexhaustible gush of alacrity, a declaration of love for someone whom she may not be seeing again unless fate had a hand in bringing them together in the future for a specific reason. But she chose not to dwell on that possibility, since none of her other given-up-for-adoption siblings had ever, by chance, reconnected with her.

While gaping at this diminutive figure, she caught sight of an awfully large one standing outside supposedly the third window in the backyard on the far-right side of the bedroom, the curtains occluding the person's face from complete view. Without hesitation, Tin crouched below the windowsill, unsure whether this person was a relative or neighbour of the family or just another outsider like her. Either way, it would be in her best interest to keep out of sight or risk being reported to the authorities. But her ever inquisitive nature only prompted her to want to find out what was keeping this other person glued to the window, so she retreated quietly, made a right turn and tiptoed behind an unbroken row of shrubs facing the third window behind which the person was positioned, hoping to gain an inkling of whatever intentions he or she might be harbouring. She reminded herself to scream with all the lung power she could muster if her instincts, which she sort of knew she could trust most of the time, were to impress upon her that the latter might be a thief planning to break into the house at such an opportune time when many would probably be out of their homes—women running errands, men working, and kids playing in the open. Even though burglary was a rare phenomenon in Lorong Limau, for obvious reasons, its existence had been reported albeit far from rampant in relatively wealthier build-ups like Kallang Gardens.

Through an opening the size of a keyhole from behind the shrubs, Tin could finally figure out the person loitering at the window was a woman. She seemed to be watching an object in the room without appearing to dwell on it for more than a few seconds, at once hesitant and attentive, juxtaposing between maintaining status quo and receding altogether, much like a burglar undecided about whether to break into the house. On the other hand, she also seemed too forlorn to possess the energy needed to be on her feet any longer than the next few minutes, let alone loot the place, her posture frail, demeanour battered. Nonetheless, Tin remained alert, continuing to watch her from a sufficient remove, all prepared to shout 'thief' over and over at the top of her voice the moment this woman decided to climb over the window into the bedroom.

In the end, she never got the chance to play heroine, for the woman did not sneak into the house. For minutes, they just held their respective positions. But something else was at play: first, it was the unmistakable fake gold ring on her finger, then the familiar fierce red of her *sarong kebaya*, and the ultimate giveaway was the recognizable manner in which she wavered in times of anxiety or uncertainty—that overall slight trembling of her body, the quick deep breaths she would take, the hand, usually the right one, she would gently press against her stomach as if to stifle the butterflies inside her gut. At first, Tin refused to believe what had since taken on an air of familiarity. She rubbed the scene from her eyes and stared again. *Isn't she supposed to be recuperating at home? Isn't she too frail to even utter a complete coherent sentence? What on earth is she doing here?* Midway through that last rhetorical question, she already had a good sense of what her mother was beholding, though not quite locating her exact trigger.

From her parents' discussions with the adoptive couple, mostly within her earshot, it had struck her that her mother had been highly apathetic, never once betraying any regret of giving up her soon-to-be-born child. Furthermore, there

had been sufficient number of proclamations made by her—
'Do what you want with the baby, I don't really care', 'No,
I won't want to see her ever'—to convince Tin that she all
but possessed nary an iota of care and love for her newborn,
which made it all the more puzzling now to see her stealthily
watching over her baby daughter. Mind-boggling for sure. Tin
also had no idea how her mother could have overcome her
feeble condition to get out of bed and travel all the way here.

The crickets chirped. The breeze came in steady bursts.
The weathervane atop one of the nearby houses stirred a
little. A couple of jackfruit trees stood out among a host of
other nameless pollarded ones. The neighbourhood remained
as quiet as ever. Had Tin actually screamed for help in the
name of burglary, chances were no one would even have
been around to respond to her calls.

She searched her mother's face for whatever semblance
of buried feelings she could find, some sign of remorse
or guilt that she might have perhaps overlooked from the
beginning. It drew a blank. However, at one juncture, she
unexpectedly bore witness to her mum's hitherto masterfully
disguised emotion: heartbreak. She recognized that look,
for she had seen it before. Every fragile bone seemed to be
bursting out of her mother's face and looked set to shatter at
any moment. She had the same countenance each time after
giving birth to stillborn babies, just before plunging into a
brief but soul-wrenching episode of caterwauling. This time
round, falling short of Tin's reckoning, she did not collapse
into a mess of heaving sobs.

For the next thirty minutes or so, Tin continued to hide
behind the hedgerow, watching her mother watch the baby
from outside the window. Struggling to continue standing

up, her mother held on to a stone pillar next to the window for physical support. It appeared as if she was about to use up the last vestige of strength any moment soon but, somehow, she managed to keep at it.

Tin could have left Kallang Gardens right there and then, cognizant of the consequences she would face for returning home late especially with Gau Pee keeping track of time while waiting for her to bring back the pig intestines so that she could proceed with her cooking. *Does Gau Pee even know that Ma is out? If so, perhaps there's no more urgency to boil the intestine soup? Or should I go home now?* In the end, she chose to linger alongside her mother unbeknownst to the latter, patiently waiting for her to finish what she had set out to accomplish. *She needs her closure as much as I do . . . I understand.*

Both mother and daughter eventually made their way back to Lorong Limau on foot—the latter trailing after the former at a safe distance—chalking up an hour and a half in travelling time. Initially, Tin was worried that her mother might not even have the stamina to walk a few metres let alone all the way to their village given that she had been bedridden for the past few days. But as they journeyed on, she was taken aback at her mother's 'miraculous recovery'. Never once did she take a break to catch her breath or rest her feet, not even for a few seconds; she simply propelled herself till she arrived home. *No, I don't think she was sick in the first place . . . she was merely suspended in grief. Now I'm beginning to see the whole picture.* On her part, Tin stayed close behind, trusting it would be her responsibility to ensure her mum reached home safely especially in her emotionally tattered state. If she happened to trip over something and fall down or collapse halfway through, Tin would immediately make her presence known and render the required assistance. But, in the end, neither did her mother need any such emergency intervention nor did she know her daughter had been following her from behind—well, it was so from Tin's perspective.

It was only years later, just before Tin's mother died of tuberculosis that the episode in Kallang Gardens was broached albeit not at length.

'I'm sorry I've not treated you well all your life. Time and again, I've scolded and beaten you for nothing,' mumbled Tin's mother on her deathbed. 'You will forgive me, won't you?'

'Ma, let's not dwell on the past,' said Tin with nothing but profound sorrow written all over her face.

'I know how much you've cared for me all this while, including the time you and I walked home from Kallang, do you remember? You must have gone there for the same reason . . . to see your little sister.' Her mother broke into a fit of coughing before taking a deep breath. 'I knew back then you were keeping a watch over me even though I pretended not to acknowledge you, yet in the end I . . . betrayed you. I'm sorry . . . yes . . . the time you carried me home . . . I'm sorry.' She said in a faint tone, struggling to remain coherent.

So, Ma knew about it after all.

'Shhh . . . it's okay Ma, it's all in the past.'

Incidentally, that last shared moment with her mother also left her with something she would carry with her for the rest of her life—her mother's advice on reconciling with loss, which, in her case, included stillborns, adoptions, and

gender inequality, among many others: you have to learn to
let go of pain and blame, the grudges and the what-should-
have-been-scenarios that come with the territory, just let
them go for your own good.

Tin set foot in the house a good fifteen minutes—deliberately
timed so as not to arouse any notion of coincidence—
following her mum's return, which had been received with
rapturous relief by everyone in the family except Tin's father
who had merely said something to the effect of, 'Gan-ni-na,
you should have come home much earlier.' She saw her family
gathered together in the living room all looking spirited and
communal. It appeared that Gau Pee and Kee Kee had been
badgering their mother into revealing her whereabouts to
which she merely gave tight-lipped responses.

'Not to worry, I'm well now. I'd simply gone for a very
long walk,' she said at one point.

The cheery vibe in the house immediately gave way to
rippling tension once Gau Pee directed her attention from
her mother to Tin. Like an executioner descending upon
the condemned, she wasted no time in accusing her younger
sister of gallivanting elsewhere when she should have
returned home straight from the market and chastising her
for allowing the pig intestines she had bought to turn putrid,
thereby flushing money down the gully as a result of her own
irresponsible behaviour.

'The intestines are still fit for consumption,' said Tin in
a calm manner.

'Don't you dare argue with me!' Gau Pee slapped Tin
hard on her left cheek. 'And where the hell were you the

whole morning?' Their two youngest siblings, Kee Kee and Bok Koon, shuddered at the sound of the smacking.

Tin did not respond, merely averting her eyes and preparing for the worst to come.

'Slap her again! She so deserves it!' Ah Hock interposed with glee, regarding Tin from a posture of sullen antagonism. In more ways than one, he and Gau Pee were rather similar. One could always count on Ah Hock to back Gau Pee up and vice-versa in the event of conspiring against others and watching them suffer. Sometimes they could be downright nasty, other times unsuspectingly conniving like during one of their relatives' wedding when both had volunteered to take photos of the celebrants together with their families and guests only to have everyone fooled in the final outcome. No films were ever loaded into the camera to begin with, which they had borrowed from Jude Vincent, the village chief. The entire undertaking was nothing but a sham. They cajoled everyone present at the wedding, including their own parents and siblings, to pose from various angles, which most people happily did, then studiously clicked away like they had taken the perfect shots, and showered them with the gushiest of compliments. In between the snapping of pictures, they looked at each other and tried not to double over with laughter. A few days after the ceremony, they took special delight in breaking the 'unfortunate' news to the couple: 'We are so sorry the film had been damaged beyond anything we can ever hope to salvage, it was defective from the beginning, something that's out of our control and we seek your understanding on this matter.'

'What are you waiting for?' Ah Hock added.

Gau Pee whacked Tin's face a couple more times. One would imagine Tin's father or mother taking charge at this point. However, they kept silent, their body language announcing nothing more loudly than their approval of Gau Pee helming the gauntlet for Tin. This was the 'betrayal' Tin's mother raised with rue prior to her passing. She could have told everyone what had happened in Kallang Gardens and most of all, she could have defended her daughter and put a stop to Gau Pee's onslaught but she did not. Lest she have to justify her sneaking out and subsequent actions, especially to her unempathetic husband, she had no desire to reveal the truth.

Resilient as ever, Tin remained largely unstirred, mostly looking down on the floor, hands gently pressing against her slightly swollen cheeks as if to disembarrass them of any further torment. Sadly, after all those physical and verbal lashings from Gau Pee, it was left to Tin's father to take up the baton. No doubt he would always be on Gau Pee's side. For the next ten minutes, he handed Tin the beating of her life—belts, canes, and all. Together with Ah Hock, Gau Pee watched from the sidelines, both of them smiling and nodding their heads in tandem while Tin's mother, Kee Kee, and Bok Koon chose to look elsewhere, anywhere except Tin's face, a taut mask of excruciation that was almost too painful to confront. Somehow, the cigarette-ash grey of the cement floor and the reflective tint of the dining table seemed to provide an odd sense of distraction if not calm for them against the ongoing truculence. They would no more have wanted to witness the beating than they would have picked up a broom and swept the floor on Chinese New Year, an act considered the mother of all taboos as far as old wives' tale was concerned.

After the beating, you would imagine Tin might have been allowed to take some time to nurse her freshly inflicted bodily wounds, but no. She was further punished by Gau Pee who demanded that she single-handedly attend to all household chores for the day including chopping the wood to start the fire, then boiling the pig intestines soup, getting the laundry done, and finally cleaning up the house.

Chapter Four

She took a look at Gau Pee and shuddered, a sharp pang of uneasiness crashing through her mind like a thunderclap. Her expression hardened as she turned to face Tin's mother who had invited her, the matchmaker, to their house with the intent of finding a husband for Gau Pee. However, Sweet Shirley, as she was normally called by everyone in her own village for her ability to sugar-coat even the worst of intentions and reasons, did manage to conquer an apparently lump-stuck throat to work her usual glibness.

'Now, tell me Mrs Chew, what type of man do you have in mind for your special girl here?' she asked, her smile widening more than usual to overcompensate for her momentary slip in decorum upon seeing Gau Pee for the first time, all three of them seated at the dining table.

'Oh, hopefully a good man,' Tin's mother replied.

'Hmm,' Sweet Shirley muttered. She stumbled upon her vocation by chance one day after listening to a girlfriend's sob story of being dumped by her boyfriend and then, not long after, introducing her to another guy, one of her distant cousins, to whom she reckoned her girlfriend would take a shine given her penchant for men who were tall and well-built and, more importantly, who would put their future wives' priorities ahead of their own. Subsequently, both parties got married after dating for a few months, her first unintended case of 'success' was followed gradually by a slew of others the moment she decided to make a living out of it. That she possessed the magnetism of a socialite helped a great deal in building up her vast network of friends and acquaintances. When she was not matchmaking, she could be seen mediating quarrels and disputes between girlfriends and boyfriends, between husbands and wives, all of which amounted to some sort of a stipend one way or another for her effort and time invested in these people's lives. She attended to the needs of both the rich and poor, charging each client discriminately according to what he or she could afford. It goes without saying that her remuneration from the likes of Tin's mother would normally amount to no more than a pittance but that hardly detracted her from wanting to spread what she believed to be the ultimate source of happiness: couplehood. Ironically, she had opted to remain single all her life, devoting herself instead to the pairing of other soulmates.

'So, I assume "good" in your vocabulary means handsome, caring, and having a respectable job? Am I right?' Sweet Shirley said with a nice and lazy smile, her thick eyelashes fluttering at every adjective. She was neither tall nor short, just the right height for a woman of her generation; neither was she pretty nor ugly, just pleasant enough to look at without getting hooked.

'Yes, that would be ideal, but of course we can do with less if you feel it's not possible,' Tin's mother affirmed.

'Ma, what do you mean by "if it's not possible"?' Gau Pee interjected with a tone that alleged her mother might be insinuating her lack of appeal and thus copping out even before any deal could be struck. Cutting a glance to her mum sitting next to her, she carved out an expression that was halfway between a scowl and a look of defeat.

Recognizing that look on her daughter's face, Tin's mother reached out for her hands, held them in hers, and said, 'Maybe I'm just not comfortable with you marrying a so-called perfect man—well you know, rich, handsome, and loving. I don't know, maybe it would not be good for you in the long run. I don't know for sure, but I've seen too many cases of women with perfect husbands ending up sad and alone if you know what I mean. Look at Minnie, your second aunt. She got married to your uncle Martin who was good-looking, came from a wealthy family, and loved your aunt so much and look what happened to her?'

'What happened?' Sweet Shirley's curiosity was piqued by and large.

'She lost her husband in an accident even before Angie, my cousin, was born,' Gau Pee replied on behalf of her mother, her tone still as icy and monotonous. 'He was struck by lightning.'

'Oh God,' Sweet Shirley muttered.

'I'd rather die than to let that happen to you,' Tin's mother said, letting go of her grip on Gau Pee's hands, trembling a little as she made that vow.

'I know,' said Gau Pee. Her annoyance was lifted from her face, replaced by a languid tenderness. Both mother and daughter looked as if they were about to embrace and have a good cry together, befitting a funeral rather than a matchmaking setting, which prompted Sweet Shirley to want to steer the conversation back to where it was supposed to be heading, but not before allowing Tin's mother to dish out one final conjecture with regards to a woman marrying her ideal man.

'And if the women don't end up being widows at a young age, they may ultimately have to put up with philandering husbands because these men can easily seduce any woman they want given their money and good looks. So, I'm not sure which is worse—a dead husband or a cheater.'

Sweet Shirley threw back her head laughing at the ridiculousness of what she would privately term small-minded make-believe only to have her light-heartedness frowned upon by a pair of unflinching countenances and immediately swallowed up by their how-dare-you-laugh-at-us rectitude.

A band of sunlight pierced through the otherwise dimly lit living quarters of Tin's mother. The three women huddled around the circular dining table in the centre of the room, each anchored by her own rumination of where she stood in relation to this get-together. For Tin's mother, it was about making sure her favourite daughter would not turn out to be a spinster and would hopefully be taken care of by a husband long after her passing; for Gau Pee, it was about marrying someone superior to Molly's future husband, whoever that might be, so she could not care less if her own husband were to die young or sow the wildest of oats or be stationed overseas as long as she herself was able to lead a more luxurious life than her next-door arch-rival. For Sweet Shirley, who was relatively free of unrealistic expectations, it might be no more of a crime to wish the best for Gau Pee obviously facing one blatant obstacle—the astoundingly pronounced shape of her nose—than it was for a village slut to single out her most memorable kiss from a plethora of men with whom she had flirted or slept. But then again, she had never quite had a reaction so strong that it stilled her breath in the most unpleasant knee-jerk manner upon seeing a client for the first time as she'd had with Gau Pee. In all fairness, the latter was not butt-ugly unlike a couple of girls she had tried to play matchmaker for throughout the years: one had teeth jutting out of her mouth like a natural carnivore, another could have suffered from some facial implosion and then there was this girl whom Sweet Shirley would consider one of God's most immaculately disproportionate creations, for she was paper-thin waist up yet had a truckload of cellulite down south. Somehow, Gau Pee was a category unto herself. She was not exactly repulsive for repulsion's sake; she had a trim figure, an average-looking face, barring that nose of hers, and a rather smooth complexion. Compared to those butt-ugly girls, you would think she ought to have a fighting chance to get married, yet something unspeakably malevolent seems to coalesce upon her the moment you catch sight of her nose.

'So, Gau Pee do you fancy any boy here in Lorong Limau?' Sweet Shirley asked, relieved to be at the helm of her game after all that blether about the fate of a woman netting a worthy catch of a husband. *Seriously, who wouldn't want a trophy man as a life partner? Perhaps only the insecure would deny themselves of this goal. In my experience, I've not once witnessed tragedy the way they described earlier when a woman marries a trophy man*, she thought to herself. Too smart and too experienced for that kind of nonsense, she steered clear of sustaining its momentum.

'I don't like the boys in this village. They're all uncouth, superficial, and block-headed. I want someone intelligent and well-mannered,' she replied with a whiff of self-entitlement.

'Hmm,' the matchmaker mused.

The truth was there had been a few guys in Lorong Limau whom Gau Pee secretly fancied. She even made the first move to get to know them, asking for their names, acting coquettishly, pretending to be kind and sincere, hoping they would be interested in her although it did not take her long to realize they were anything but. In a few cases, they befriended her with the aim of wanting to be introduced to her more affable and attractive neighbour, not knowing she and Molly were in fact nemeses, which had all the more caused her to seethe with relentless anger.

'Gau Pee is a very special girl. She's hard-working, resourceful, in fact half our family income stems from her resourcefulness. She's good at cooking and baking, she makes nice clothes for other people, she does all the housework in my absence, and she's a real beauty,' Tin's mother exclaimed. At the sound of the last description, Sweet Shirley once again felt a thickening in her throat, a constriction as if she might actually cry. Was she hearing it right? 'A real beauty'? There was no denying every mother would think the best of her children, but this was way beyond preposterous. That Tin's mother was able to keep a straight face while uttering those words made her realize how insane and grandly absurd this woman was turning out to be. With Gau Pee nodding coyly in agreement, Sweet Shirley felt as if the proverbial sound made by her heart, could it speak, would be similar to that of a tree trunk fracturing and falling to earth in slow motion.

The tree finally landed in a seismic thud when Gau Pee said, 'Oh Ma, you don't have to speak the obvious. I'm sure Aunty Shirley here has eyes to vouch for the facts.' She eyed the matchmaker, weighing her reaction with a catty grin.

Sweet Shirley decided it would be in her best interest not to deny Gau Pee and her mother the pleasure of acquiescence lest they say nasty things about her and jeopardize her favourable standing in the industry. She also thought it would be more politically correct to let the men she would introduce to Gau Pee in time execute the harsh but necessary task of refuting Gau Pee's wildly inflated notion of her own appeal, instead of she herself delivering the judgement.

'Mrs Chew, you're indeed one lucky mother to have such a beautiful, talented daughter!' Sweet Shirley clutched at her pearl necklace as she thrusted the compliment out of her system.

The weight of the day seemed to stack heavily, burgeoning upon her nerves, a day when so many things could go right— well, right for everyone except her. At the entrance to Ruby Theatre, a mere fifteen minutes' walk from Lorong Limau, Molly was waiting for her date to show up. This also happened to be the third time she would be meeting up with yet another stranger, a potential husband if all things were to go well, (no) thanks to Sweet Shirley whose services her mum had been proactively engaging similar to what Tin's mother was doing for Gau Pee. Deep down inside, she had never been comfortable under the auspices of matchmaking—the initial profiling, the exchange of photos, the forced awkwardness when both parties finally meet and then the hastily arranged marriage on the basis of mutual attraction no matter how minuscule. But, at the same time, neither would she openly fend off her mum's good intentions knowing it would only cause her unbearable pain, more often than not awash in tears and faux-suicide attempts, at the admission of raising an unfilial daughter who would dare challenge her mother's noble objective of finding her a worthy, deserving husband.

'I believe I'll meet someone by chance one day, fall in love, and get married. I don't want marriage to be reduced to some form of transaction, which is what matchmaking is all about,' Molly had been iterating to Tin for quite a while now. For better or worse, instead of showing defiance in the presence of her mum, she would rather mangle the outcome of her dates set up by Sweet Shirley as she had done in her last two arranged meetings by pretending to be a natural born glutton in the first and a steadfast nose-picker in the other.

'You seem to enjoy food quite a lot, don't you?' the guy in the first meeting had asked. In response, Molly simply glared at him with her mouth open, its cavity filled to the brim with chunks of roasted pork buns, displaying on purpose her displeasure at being gastronomically interrupted, and then gave a slight nod and continued chewing and swallowing, followed by yet another round of squeezing more food into her mouth. At their rendezvous, a neighbourhood coffee shop selling light snacks and beverages, Molly and her date could be seen occupying a table in the far-right corner, the former devouring pork buns and washing them down with coffee, the latter watching and fidgeting at the sight of this very woman showing neither grace nor restraint and who would in all likelihood put on weight rather quickly given how much food she could squeeze into her mouth at one go. A potentially fat, unmannered, not to mention financially-draining—he guessed he would probably have to pay double for food to have her around—wife was the complete opposite of what he was seeking, so much so that both their names were never spoken of again in the same breath by the matchmaker after their initial meeting.

On her next date, Molly decided to ratchet up the gross factor by picking her nose non-stop in front of the guy and then flicking off the gloop one by one from her fingers with absolutely no regards to where they might land—his food, his face, it did not matter. The guy bailed out halfway through, claiming he had a stomach ache and leaving thereafter in a hurry. 'I kept patting his arm after each picking till he just couldn't take it any more and I think my snot may have been stuck somewhere in his hair follicles,' Molly recounted the story to Tin, which kept them in stitches.

On her third date this morning, she had arrived earlier not because she was eager to meet the guy—oh no, not at all, that could not be any further from the truth—but she had wanted to leave the house as swiftly and quietly as possible so as to avoid well wishes from her family members, especially her mother. 'All the best my pretty one,' she would say to her daughter, 'and be sure to be on your best manners.'

It was about half past eight, the humidity in the air already palpable. Not a soul was loitering around Ruby Theatre where she had been waiting for the guy to show up, understandably so as morning screening of movies was simply unheard of at that time with the first show normally commencing at five o'clock in the evening. Here at Ruby, the shutter was still down, its lobby strewn with litter by moviegoers from the night before—sweet wrappers, food crumbs, ticket stubs, *kacang puteh* paper cones. There was even a pair of white panties spotted at the far end of the lobby near the staircase leading to the pricier seats upstairs. Obviously, someone must have forgotten to put it back on after making out. It was not unusual then for couples who were dating, many of whom would not be able to afford a meal together at any indoor eatery, let alone book a motel room, to conduct their clandestine sexual escapades in places like movie theatres, since the price of a ticket was cheaper than a bowl of noodles in a coffee shop. And if the show being screened was unpopular, which meant the theatre would be relatively empty, couples could by all means let their hands and mouths roam free. Some would canoodle in near darkness only to hold their breath and come to a momentary halt whenever light from the movie screen—sunshine, outdoor scenery, a drastic transition from dimly-lit to sparkling bright scenes— cast itself on the audience. After the movie, a few couples might linger surreptitiously in the darker recesses of the lobby to further exploit their marathon appetite, some even staying beyond closing time with the shutter down and lights off and subsequently making their way out through the fire escape, a small opening on the theatre rooftop, after claiming the whole nine yards of horniness.

Molly tittered at the sight of the panties. She wondered if she might one day find herself in a sexually enterprising situation, lying on the lobby floor, legs spread out and hung aloft the guy's shoulders, breasts tumbling back and forth in a swirl, sweat glistening on her body as he drilled her over and over with unrelenting concupiscence. She imagined Bette Davis and Anne Baxter peering disapprovingly at her from the *All About Eve* marquee hanging four-square from the ceiling in the lobby. She imagined having to confess to her mother (since her father was mostly at sea and absent from their lives ten out of twelve months a year) about her pregnancy once she started to show. She imagined being disowned and kicked out of the house, left to fend for herself and the baby, since the guy who had sex with her in the theatre lobby would probably be too poor, too young, and too scared to assume the responsibilities of fatherhood. She imagined growing haggard and wrinkled as a result of taking on two or three jobs in order to make ends meet. *Oh no, this is too much*, she said to herself. *Maybe it's best that I wait till after marriage to have sex. Or maybe not. I don't know, really.*

For every guy who happened to be within twenty to thirty feet of the theatre, she began searching in each of their faces for some resemblance with what she recalled of her date's countenance captured on a photograph shown to her and her mother by Sweet Shirley during one of the latter's visits to their home. In the same instance, she wondered if she could convincingly twitch one of her eyes with abandonment so as to push him away in record time. The fact that she did not like what she saw in the photo further strengthened her resolve to make an agglomeration out of this meeting. She thought he might have been cursed with oversized eyelids preventing him from opening his eyes to the fullest.

True to her expectation, the guy appeared chronically lethargic as if he had been suffering from lack of sleep and had the look of anaemia, probably due to working far too long in enclosed sunless places. He had relatively thin lips, slightly protruding ears and the smile of a pervert. And like some people who unknowingly flaunt their liabilities, he chose to display his bony arms matted with thick curly hair by wearing a short-sleeved shirt visibly soaked with perspiration by the time he sat down opposite Molly in a quiet coffee shop next to Ruby Theatre.

Across the street, the guy's parents were conducting a stakeout, hiding behind a row of street vendors selling takeaway, like fried carrot cake and red bean pancakes, and secretly eyeing Molly for any trace of odd behaviour. As first impressions went, they apparently liked what they saw so they did not stick around longer than five to ten minutes, completely missing out on the barrage of antics their prospective daughter-in-law was about to display soon after her order of coffee and toast was served.

'Wow you're very pretty, as pretty as what I saw in the photo,' he said, obviously referring to the picture he had seen courtesy of Sweet Shirley.

'Really?' Molly replied, twitching her right eye and drinking her coffee in one swoop.

At first, he thought it was merely a speck of dust trapped in her eye that might have provoked the twitching but after fifteen minutes of persistent fibrillations on her part, he was left with no redoubt against what he would consider an unacceptable physical defect. The smile on his face swiftly faded. Gone was his desire to ask more questions in order to get to know her better. All in all, he simply could not imagine a future with her as his wife. The thought of being continuously judged and talked about by strangers in public every time they would walk down the street hand-in-hand, putting on an unintended freak show, would remain Molly's strongest yet coup de grâce. He wondered why Sweet Shirley had not apprised him of Molly's eye-twitching because if she had been more responsible and truthful as a matchmaker, he would not have wasted his time taking leave of absence from work and travelling all the way from his house in Outram to Ruby Theatre, chalking up to more than an hour of a bus ride. Likewise, it would have saved his parents from making a trip here.

What also unsettled him was that Molly seemed to be experiencing some sort of inexplicable pain as well as pleasure as she spoke about her impoverished childhood, hands flailing, voice leaping into a falsetto and then breaking off with either a laugh or faux sob, her right eye twitching in sync with every last word of her every sentence, and the vacillation between these dual states of emotion seemed to make her more incoherent than ever as she started slurping her coffee so awfully loud that any lizards and cockroaches in the coffee shop would have scrambled towards their hideouts without hesitation. He too scrambled out of the place not too long after that, similar to what her previous dates had done, certain that he would not want another woman given over to histrionics in his household considering his mother alone was enough to drive him up the wall with her unpredictable, over-the-top behaviour.

After his departure, Molly burst into laughter, savouring the full deliciousness of the misadventure she had inflicted on him. Did she even feel a tad sorry for him? Maybe a little. But all things considered, she was glad to have yet again punctured her prospect of getting hitched via matchmaking. To her own astonishment, she still could not believe she had put on such a convincing performance—the twitching of the eye, the all-too-dramatic overtures, the slurping at which she herself would have flinched under normal circumstances— so much so that he had scampered off within the fastest time ever among her dates. Somehow, she had a rather compelling feeling that after this latest debacle, Sweet Shirley would now think twice about matching her with another guy, for no matchmaker, not even the most patient ones, would want to risk being reproached for suppressing the 'truth' about the girl in the marital equation. For all she knew, the guys and their respective families might have even yelled at her before slamming their doors in her face. *Poor Sweet Shirley, I don't mean to pile my shit on you*, Molly laughed while entertaining that thought.

As expected, the matchmaker did eventually inform Molly's mother a few days after the third date that she would not be sullying her reputation beyond what had already been besmirched, politely giving her a lowdown on her daughter's waggish attempts at usurping all that time and effort she had spent trying to find her the right man. Sweet Shirley, in her parting gesture, also advised Molly's mother to simply let things be.

'I have a feeling your daughter just wants to either fall in love by chance or remain a spinster throughout her life,' Sweet Shirley said without a hint of rancour.

Taking that advice to heart, Molly's mother decided to surrender to the whim of the universe by allowing Molly to forge her own marital future. If nothing, she could only hope her daughter's life would turn out much better than hers.

Finally. A miracle. Who could have believed it?

This would be the first time a guy had agreed to meet up with Gau Pee after viewing her photo without experiencing qualmishness over the shape of her nose. It was also the first time no unkind words had been uttered in the presence of the matchmaker unlike too many past occasions when the guys' parents would say something to the effect of, 'Oh my, are you kidding me? I would rather my son marry a cripple than a witch' or 'No sane parents will ever permit their son to settle for an evil-looking yokel like this one'. No surprise here—Sweet Shirley had since considered Gau Pee a forgone case given all the wretched responses thus far. So, when she first heard the words 'she looks nice' coming from a guy who could rival the best of trophy husbands, her senses immediately sought out the minor permutations, the imperceptible occult shifts in the air, those signals that would make her pinch herself into full consciousness just to confirm she wasn't dreaming at all.

At the very outset of her discussion with every guy whom she planned to introduce to Gau Pee, to ensure they would not take it amiss when they finally got to see her photo, specifically that big hook nose of hers, Sweet Shirley had to tread warily and give the marked minefields a wide berth—some parents may take offence and question why she would even attempt to introduce such a maleficent-looking woman to their sons—by upholding the caveat that it was only her duty as a matchmaker to provide people with as many options as possible ranging from the popular to the leftovers. Of course, she would not dare articulate the term 'leftovers' during any of her meetings with the parents, as it would only sound demeaning. They would also think that if she could label someone else's son or daughter as a leftover, she might say the same thing about theirs to another person. As a respected professional, Sweet Shirley would instead use the phrase 'here are the ones for mass consideration' to introduce the likes of Gau Pee via photos. By that, people would understand that the prospects do not (and cannot) belong to the category of select prized pickings, which basically mirrors reality: the world is made up of average-looking people who far outnumber the beautiful. A less politically correct way of saying it would be 'eight or nine out of ten are either average-looking or ugly'.

'I like her,' said the guy, reposed and stately, 'Hmm, what do you think?' He passed the photo to his mother who then shared it with his father, both peering at the image as if they were silently reading a poem together. Sweet Shirley came within an inch of losing her sanity the moment they smiled and nodded their heads in approval for she could not believe that they would pay Gau Pee's nose no more attention than a puff of breath. The self-coined phrase 'ding dong the witch is not dead' riffed through her mind teetering on the brink of lunacy. She smiled at them nervously.

Chapter Five

The wind distended Tin's hair in small black tufts around her ears and she pressed it back gently with one hand, the other holding an empty pail to be filled with water at the village's water collection point, made possible by a faucet linked via underground pipes to several wells in its milieu. Every household was entitled to free water, its members queuing up with containers and pails every morning, waiting for Jude Vincent, the village head, a retired civil servant who was known to put on a happy face in front of acquaintances and strangers and reserve his crankier side for people he knew well and loved, to unlock the metallic enclosure around the faucet so that they could fill up their buckets with water and then gingerly carry them back to their homes, hopefully with minimal spillage, for consumption, baths, ablutions, and whatever else they needed of it. Sometimes one may have to queue up for a good thirty minutes or more just to obtain a pail of water owing to the sheer number of residents thronging the collection point.

'Patience!' Jude Vincent would often bellow above the din, reminding everyone to keep in line and wait for their turn in a composed manner.

Tin had arrived early so, luckily, she was not too far down the queue with about seven persons ahead of her. She was keeping a lookout for Molly who seemed to be running a little late that morning.

Where the faucet was located stood Gau Pee, having ingratiated herself with Jude Vincent by delivering butter tarts to him free of charge each time she made them, thereby gradually earning the friendship of the village head who had since given her a duplicate key to the water point and officially appointed her to unlock the faucet whenever his lacerating lower back got the better of him, an injury sustained from a *parang* gash while serving as a soldier fighting the Japanese who had invaded Singapore during World War II. Jude Vincent had also made it a point to do Gau Pee the courtesy of disregarding her publicly beleaguered subject of a nose, focusing instead on her insatiable appetite for hard work, for establishing her own brand of leadership in Lorong Limau and not least for making those delectable butter tarts that had simply held his palate hostage. To the very few like her sister Tin and her bête noire Molly, who could easily see through her humbuggery, the way she had garnered the trust and support of the likes of Jude Vincent, it was no surprise that each step taken by her in the name of self-advancement would always bear its expected fruit and that every coincidence she encountered would somehow feel preordained one way or another. They could also tell she was gunning for something beyond faucet control—she wanted her opinions to hold sway over Jude

Vincent concerning major decisions executed on behalf of all villagers.

'Would it be all right if I were to come back here with another pail without having to queue up all over again?' asked a certain young boy whose halitosis was as bona fide a cachet as his lack of ill manners. 'I would be very grateful but if it's not possible, I totally understand.' He appeared respectful of Gau Pee, bowing gently as he presented his supplication.

'Well, of course you can. I know you have to help your father in his carpentry, so I guess you wouldn't want to spend time queuing up one more time after you've filled up your first pail of water, am I right? Well, let's just say it'll be my pleasure to assist in any way,' Gau Pee replied with a touch of fabricated verve.

'Thank you, thank you, thank you so much. You're ever so considerate towards me and my family,' said the boy, bowing repeatedly as he lifted his pail filled to the brim with water and trudged away.

Oh my, for all his social grace, he barely has the decency to expunge that odour from his breath! Gau Pee phrased the words in her mind. *Anyway, in time to come, I'm sure we're going to have furniture given to us for free as a result of my kindness.* With that, she unknowingly flashed an evil grin.

She caught sight of Tin and summoned her to come over with a wave of her hand. However, Tin chose not to budge, as she felt it would be unfair to jump queue just because her sister was now managing the water collection point. Gau Pee responded with a glower verging on a no-holds-barred causticity, openly demonstrating to Tin that she found her behaviour far from acceptable, an unexpected defiance that would both skin her ego and ratchet up the humiliation quotient in public, something she simply could not tolerate. She had to do something fast to assert her queen bee persona.

'Here! Now!' Gau Pee hollered, repeatedly pointing her index finger downwards in a hostile show of authority, causing others in the queue to stop whatever they were chatting about and direct their attention, albeit briefly, towards her, a firebrand who was reportedly known not to grovel, not even to thugs and Neanderthals in the village, a trait Tin would also subsequently acquire and put to good use in her formative years as a wife and mother.

Chastened, Tin begrudgingly made her way past the people ahead of her in the queue to where Gau Pee was standing with arms akimbo, every sinew, every muscle, every lymph node, and every nerve of hers becoming stiffer as the distance between them narrowed. While her fear of being blown up in her face by Gau Pee might not be unfounded, her concern about upsetting others as a result of her jumping queue was anything but. For one, these people had known better than to offend Gau Pee given her reputation. So, all they did was merely watch her blaze in her cold, divine glory like bystanders observing a firing squad helmed by an imperious despot.

'Don't you ever dare make me shout at you again for nothing!' Gau Pee growled at Tin, their noses almost touching as if she were about to devour her sister. 'Now, top up your pail and come back for a second round minus the queuing.'

'It's just not fair to everyone else,' Tin responded, shaking her head in subtle disapproval while squatting on her haunches and filling up her pail with water. The faucet did not seem to be functioning full-throttle this morning for some unknown reason, the water trickling away instead of flowing down, hence it was taking longer than usual to get a container or pail topped up. In times like this, Jude Vincent would invariably blame it on the moon. 'It must be the low tide caused by the gravitational pull of the moon,' he would say.

'I'm the leader here and I have every right to do whatever I want,' Gau Pee said emphatically.

'You may be the leader but that doesn't give you the right to play God,' Tin gently retorted under her breath, thinking Gau Pee would not be able to hear her but the words did not escape her sister, conniving creature that she was, who gave a murmur of laughter at the sally. She took it as a compliment for she felt like God right there and then, subverting her intractable sibling and along with it the latter's moral weight which struck her more like sententiousness than anything else.

'Where's Kee Kee? I thought she's supposed to be with you?' Gau Pee asked.

'She said she's not feeling well, you know, the same old excuse,' Tin muttered.

'Why can't you be more sympathetic towards her? She's young and frail and usually indisposed so the least we can do as older sisters is to show more understanding,' Gau Pee said, mocking Tin for her lack of empathy although in private she could not have been more aligned with the truth, knowing how Kee Kee had for the longest time managed to eschew household chores. Of course, her bias had something to do with the fact that the youngest member of their family was always in cahoots with her on almost every discourse, every subject matter of contention.

At that point, without warning, Molly sidled up to them from nowhere with two containers. She mouthed a merry 'hi' to Tin and nodded nonchalantly at Gau Pee. Making good on her usual pact with Tin—whoever arrived earlier would reserve a slot in the queue for the other—she automatically assumed her place beside Tin ready to fill up her containers.

'Wait a minute . . . who gives you the right to jump queue?' Gau Pee blustered, deliberately putting her foot between Molly and the faucet so as to stop her from collecting any water. Tin glared at her helplessly, neither able to defend her friend from Gau Pee's distaste nor adopt the latter's rebuff as a collective justification for herself; she was merely waiting for the right time to chip in.

'What kind of question is that? You know fully well that Tin and I always *chope* a space for each other if one of us happens to come a bit earlier,' Molly responded unequivocally, stressing on the word 'chope', local argot for 'reserve' or 'stake out'.

'Well then, let me ask you. Is your surname Chew? No? I don't think so, which means you're not part of my family and which means you don't have the privilege to jump queue here unlike Tin who's my beloved sister, so you might as well drop all that *choping* excuse and start queuing up from behind,' Gau Pee said, her voice dripping with sarcasm, her grin etched in nothing less than unadulterated malice. Coincidentally, both Tin and Molly cringed in unison when Gau Pee uttered 'beloved'.

'I really don't have all the time in the world to argue with you,' Molly said, nudging Gau Pee's leg aside without hesitation and waiting anxiously for Tin to complete her task so that she could start hers. Gau Pee bristled and was about to cast aspersions on her when her sister interjected.

Commiserating with Molly, Tin added dispassionately, 'Gau Pee, since Kee Kee is not here to offer her help, Molly is the only one I can count on to collect water on our behalf in addition to doing so for her own family. I'm sure you understand.'

'You stay out of this!' she snapped at Tin who managed to remain stolid, being more or less inured to Gau Pee's outbursts over the years. Turning to Molly, she remarked with a smirk, 'I can sense your frustration but don't even think of venting it on me just because you've been having an awful time with all the dates Sweet Shirley set up for you. I mean, seriously, who can blame the guys for running away from you? I would probably act the same way if I were in their shoes.'

Molly simply ignored her, focusing instead on filling up the first of two large wooden containers. Besides, she was not in the mood to joust with Gau Pee, as she had to hurry home to execute her usual slew of chores from cooking to laundry.

While waiting in line, the rest of the villagers simply had not much to do except to watch what they perceived as a couple of termagants—Gau Pee and company, that is— trade barbs over the most trivial of matters that they would subsequently poach for tattle with their own families and friends. If not much else, it offered them a much-needed distraction from waiting with battered patience for their turns at the faucet owing to a terribly feeble discharge from the wells that morning. They also had to put up with an escalating humidity that was no less anathematic. The sun had since ascended mid-sky, turning the surface of water puddles orange, burning red on the white corrugated tin rooftops of buildings and bathing the trees in fiery warmth.

Still on the subject of matchmaking, Gau Pee continued to jab Molly by vaunting her prospect of tying the nuptial knot much quicker than her arch-rival would, claiming she would be meeting her potential husband in a few days' time, a man who she emphatically mentioned had been swooning over her beauty to no end since catching a glimpse of her photograph according to what she had heard from Sweet Shirley. Molly and Tin once again winced in perfect harmony, this time rolling their eyes in addition to shooting each other a conspiratorial smile. But neither of them was prepared for what was about to follow: a spurt of pathogens fired off from Gau Pee's mouth to momentarily incapacitate even the most stoic of pilgrims in any odyssey.

'I think you're cursed in life just like your pathetic mum. Tsk, tsk, tsk, that's so sad,' Gau Pee said, her expression straddling between astringency and mock sympathy.

Molly, by now filling up her second container, stared at Gau Pee and questioned assertively, 'What do you mean by that?'

'Like I said, it must be a genetic curse. Well, let's face it. I suspect no man will stay by your side for very long whether you eventually get married or not. Look at your parents, for example. A part of me thinks your dad has become a deckhand simply because he regrets marrying someone like your mum who's basically gutless and then having a tramp of a daughter like you so I can perfectly understand why he would prefer to be anywhere except in his own home most of the time. I mean who can blame him for escaping from such a toxic, miserable environment?' Gau Pee answered with a sharp laugh followed purposefully by a sigh of lament.

'Speak for yourself, you bloody bitch!' Molly shouted. She stood up with one of her containers and splashed the water on Gau Pee, drenching her from head to toe. Hardly ever at the water collection, normally dominated by the vapid act of queuing and pockets of compulsive chatter about who-had-been-spotted-at-the-brothel and whose-daughter-in-law-covered-up-her-broken-birth-month, had a public fallout been so dramatically hewed that everyone at the scene was immediately seized by wordlessness to the point where one could almost feel the surrounding temperature dropping a few degrees in a matter of milliseconds. The incisive breathless silence was however short-lived. No sooner had Tin uttered 'oh' in half-stupefaction, half-delectation than the two women in closest proximity to her lunged at each other, pulling hair, smacking faces, and accidentally snapping buttons off each other's samfu tops.

Seeing this, Tin attempted to tear Molly away from Gau Pee, grabbing her waist with both hands and pulling her in a backward motion but she was no more able to break Molly's iron-clad grip on her equally tenacious sister than Sweet Shirley was able to cogently turn Gau Pee from a schlock into a prized specimen in the eyes of prospective grooms no matter all the hard-selling. It was not until one of the guys in the queue, a strapping twenty-something son of a butcher living three doors down the corridor from Jude Vincent, yanked Gau Pee from behind that the tussle between the two women finally disassembled.

Hair dishevelled, faces flushed, samfu flaps turned inside, to say nothing of subjecting the public to exposed collarbones and bra straps, both brawlers appeared too enraged to be disconcertingly embarrassed by their own behaviour. During that era, it was largely considered unbecoming for women to fight in public and to crown it all, have their flap buttons shamelessly ripped out even though thankfully the area of fleshy exposure was confined to only their clavicles. Women in general, rich or poor, fledgling or fossil, were expected to project a genteel, august image at all times, not only a deliberate foil to their obstreperous male counterparts but also a societal sublimation of gender roles. For instance, it would be plebeian for women to eat heartily in public, ironic as it might be, since a sizeable proportion of them lived in poverty and would naturally regard engorging as a reflex to their state of being. Instead, they had to avail themselves as sparingly as possible of the spread on a table and let the men gorge with impunity.

If Tin's and Molly's mothers had been present at the scene and witnessed the contretemps, they would have collapsed out of sheer ignominy, thinking how they could ever hope to marry off their nubile daughters in the wake of such stigmatization. Already a few women, especially the older ones, at the water collection point were gasping in shock, a few others frowning with hostility at Gau Pee and Molly, fodder nonetheless ripe enough for village gossip. However, to some of the guys, the whole episode—the unravelling, the torn and wet clothes, the mere sight of two women slugging it out—felt more like a sexual intoxicant, a route to their innermost fantasies, a jolt of the abstract that stood entirely outside their own experience, marital and otherwise, conjuring up a seduction more vertiginous than anything they would dare initiate with their wives, girlfriends, or whores. Not until Molly stormed off in a huff did their erogenous locomotive finally run out of puff.

'Wait for me,' Tin cried out and went after Molly, one hand holding a pail of water and the other a pair of empty containers belonging to her friend, somewhat relieved to get away from her sister as well as the crowd that had since thickened at the collection point.

Soaked to the skin, barely able to fasten her samfu flap, Gau Pee resumed her duty with enthusiasm anew as though the catfight was nothing but a canard, a figment of her imagination where she had been compelled to bear false witness against herself. But beneath the prevailing veneer of ardour lay a seething cauldron of resentment and blame. She was just as furious with the one who had splashed water on her as she was with Tin whom she felt had been favouring kith over kin not only in this particular incident but in all matters past. She wondered what it would take for her sibling to stand on her side for once instead of invariably hurtling to her friend's defence. *In the first place, if she'd heeded my instruction not to allow Molly to join her in the queue, all this wouldn't have happened. I swear I'll get my sweet revenge on both of them one day, just you wait and see,* she mentally groused while smiling at the person—the butcher's son who had helped stop the fight—collecting his share of water.

Incidentally, months from now, Gau Pee and Molly would again cross swords, this time over a guy they both fell in love with. And the end result would be far from tidy.

Marriage to her had always felt like a competition: whoever among peers gets married first wins the game. On top of that, it has to qualify as a ticket to a better life so anyone who marries an impecunious slob not only loses but loses incontrovertibly. In Gau Pee's eyes, no one could have gone out of her way to degrade herself more shamelessly than by rushing to the altar to start a new chapter in life rooted in poverty. She would never under any circumstances allow that to happen to her. *Never*, she swore.

As she sat in the coffee shop waiting for her prospective husband, the gentleman whom Sweet Shirley had claimed to be smitten by her from just one look at her photograph,

Gau Pee studied her face on a compact borrowed from her mother, daubing more powder on her cheeks and mostly on her protuberant nose. Yes, she thought she looked beautiful. How could she not? She was all gussied up, thanks to yet another borrowed item, this time a dress from the closet of Pao, her one and only older sister who was now married to a wealthy man from another village and had since begun to sequester herself from her own impoverished family, something her husband had insisted she comply with in order to—in his own words—preserve their societal standing, much to the untold woebegoneness of Tin's parents.

'Please choose what you need quickly and leave the house before he comes back,' Pao had told Gau Pee in a simultaneously courteous and desperate manner while the latter was picking dresses and accessories from the former's wardrobe. She had arranged for Gau Pee to drop by at her house specifically when her husband was out at work, but it never occurred to her that her sister would be trying on every dress and matching it with every necklace or pair of earrings so much so that they lost track of time until it was close to five o'clock and she suddenly realized her husband would be making his way back home shortly.

'Don't rush me or I'll just continue to take my own sweet time,' Gau Pee had said defiantly. 'You ought to know this is an important milestone in my life so just buzz off and I promise I'll be out of your place before your hubby shows up.'

'Okay, okay,' Pao had replied with whispery caution, as afraid to offend her sister in the present time as she had been all those years living in the same household with her. 'But no matter what, you have to leave in the next half hour, I beg of you.'

In the end, Gau Pee had deliberately stayed on till Pao's husband came back, as she could not wait to relish a couple's fight. Once that happened, she felt a flutter in her heart only to quietly depart from the scene midway through.

At the coffee shop, she was all set to make a pretty first impression, caparisoned with gold earrings and a shimmering jade necklace which had obviously been gleaned from Pao's lavish jewellery collection. The first fifteen minutes breezed past with the guy nowhere to be seen, followed by another plodding thirty minutes of frustrating wait. Against her better judgement, she stayed for about an hour with a mere cup of black coffee to last her that entire time. The proprietor of the shop, an outwardly morose-looking but truly soft-spoken man in his sixties, had earlier been informed by Tin's mother that her daughter would be meeting her potential husband in his coffee shop so he extended the courtesy of allowing Gau Pee to occupy her seat for as long as she needed without chivvying her to order another cup of coffee as he normally would with other customers, not that she could afford it either. In the end, her date never showed up.

Perplexed and disappointed, Gau Pee walked home like a dog with its tail between the legs. Even though the reason behind his no-show could not be intuited, she felt like she had been rejected all over again, like the many times when guys had chosen Molly over her to sit with at a Chinese street opera or to play chess or badminton with or to simply offer a sweet. Even with Molly out of the picture, she was still being denied any romantic if not social endorsement. It was with affliction that she recalled this particular boy from another village, a fine swimmer, rather wealthy and handsome as well, telling her—after she had made known to him how much she adored him—that he would rather marry a crocodile than wade into matrimonial waters with her. Following that, she had single-handedly plotted that guy's fall from grace, perpetuating a rumour that he had been molesting young girls by pretending to accidentally touch their breasts or rub his thighs against theirs especially on crowded buses, mongered to unprecedented levels with the police catching wind of it and calling him up for interrogation. She even managed to bribe if not bully a few girls into substantiating the rumour-turned-accusation. Of course, the police could not unearth any concrete evidence to formally prosecute him but by then his reputation was already sullied beyond expiation and he was ultimately ostracized by relatives and friends alike and permanently blacklisted off every matchmaker's roster. The last she had heard, his parents had sent him overseas under the guise of pursuing further studies when in fact it was just an excuse for him to escape from all the subcutaneous allegations directed at him.

Putting this entire episode on rewind mode was making her more pensive than she had already been since leaving the coffee shop. She suddenly felt so weak that she had to will herself to keep walking or she might not have been able to make it back home in time for lunch. But as much as she could not care to admit, she seemed to be dragging her feet for no apparent reason other than feeling sorry for herself.

When she finally reached home, she found her mother and younger sister Kee Kee waiting for her, obviously gripped by anticipation and clearly as excited about receiving a first-hand account of what had transpired as they were about the prospect of another wedding taking place in their family less than a year after Pao's. And it was believed that there was nothing more auspicious than a wedding ceremony in a Chinese household, save the birth of babies, to usher in good tidings for everyone in the family—hopefully more money, better living conditions and eternal pink of health.

'So, how was it?' Kee Kee was the first to question, wide-eyed and gushing in delight.

'Yes, tell us, how did it go?' Tin's mother anxiously jumped on the bandwagon before Gau Pee even had the chance to respond, grabbing her daughter's hands and smiling nervously at her.

'Ma, I don't think I'm ever going to get married,' Gau Pee answered in a cracked, shaky voice. In a rare display of vulnerability, she hugged her mother who hugged her back even more tightly, blubbering in her embrace. Even Kee Kee, who would normally seize the opportunity in times like this to offer her *royal* advice ('I shall punish those who have hurt you, I will command the King's army to hunt down the traitor.') as though she were playing the role of a real princess, was taken aback by her sister's outpouring of sorrow and knew better than to not rein in the kibitzer in her.

It was not until three days later that Tin's mother and Gau Pee found out the truth from Sweet Shirley. The matchmaker had specially dropped by at their place to deliver the news while making her usual rounds in Lorong Limau. After exchanging a few sentences of no consequence, she and Tin's mother sat down to start talking about the elephant in the room. Before they could do so, Gau Pee emerged from the kitchen

to acknowledge their visitor. At this point, Sweet Shirley
appeared visibly disturbed as though she just encountered a
ghost even though she had already seen Gau Pee a couple of
times before.

*No doubt about it, she's a jinx or nothing of this magnitude
could have happened.* Of course, Sweet Shirley uttered those
words only in her head for obvious reasons. Even though
she thought Gau Pee was squarely blameworthy for what
she was about to reveal, she could not help but feel a little
sorry for her.

'You must have something important to tell us,
I know it,' Tin's mother said in a manner that smacked of
helpless urgency.

'Uh, I just came from his place, and I, uh, don't know how
to say this,' she responded, trying to steady her composure.

Prior to this, Sweet Shirley had paid a visit to the family
of the guy for whom Gau Pee had waited in vain at the coffee
shop. She was utterly shocked to hear from his parents that
he had since passed on. According to them, he was knocked
down by a bus on his way to meet up with Gau Pee that day,
catching his last breath on the tarmac and extinguishing what
might have qualified as the only fighting chance Gau Pee
would ever have in terms of fulfilling her conjugal dream,
not least her target of a wealthy spouse.

'I'm afraid, uh, to tell you that Frankie, the guy with
whom I'd set up your daughter, has died,' Sweet Shirley
muttered, looking at Tin's mother and then at Gau Pee.
After sharing with them a few details of the accident, she
did not know exactly how to offer her consolation—whether
she should cry along with them if they were to start crying,

or if she should dangle another prospect although it would be challenging to find someone else who was interested in Gau Pee, since this was the first time a tragedy as such had manifested in her matchmaking career.

Tin's mother broke down as if she were mourning the passing of her own child; Gau Pee remained rather stoic while listening to Sweet Shirley talk more about the accident, a pointed departure from the heavy-heartedness she had displayed on the day she walked home from the coffee shop. To the matchmaker's surprise, Gau Pee even brushed aside the matter like it did not bother her.

'Well, I consider it his loss not to have met me. Anyway, I've got more important things right now to attend to,' she said in a tone that was dry, almost disengaged, and she marched back to the kitchen.

She would remain a lovelorn spinster all her life, a rather bitter one, consistently mocking women who got married and in her later years, doing her darn best to stir trouble for couples whenever she could if not break them up without a whit of contrition. She would fabricate stories that would pit husbands against wives, girlfriends against boyfriends, even mothers-in-law against daughters-in-law often resulting in tensions, quarrels, and fights among these married couples, and she would ruck up her shoulders that nearly touched her ears like a kid bestowed with the perfect birthday present whenever she witnessed one half of a dyad inveighing against the other, more often than not a direct consequence of her concocted wiles and lies. And when the situation became irreparable, she would secretly raise her hands and proclaim, 'God is fair.'

But karma would often have a pachydermatous memory for any jab or wrongdoing, significant and otherwise, something she may have failed to grasp while happily setting up Tin for a beating by their father or scoffing at others' good fortune or thwarting the union of souls. As karma would have it, she would remain a steadfast virgin cursed with the ruthless solitude of a loveless life.

Chapter Six

'It's heading our way!' shouted one of the neighbours, a fat woman living a few doors down the corridor from Tin's family.

'Time to cook up a storm!' echoed another neighbour, this time a mother whose prodigious childbearing had left no mark on her narrow waist and handsome hips much to the envy of other women. She had produced nine children within a period of seven years.

Like her, many matriarchs would race ahead of one another to start cooking upon witnessing the sky aswirl with scudding dark clouds, thinking to themselves that they had better not rule out the possibility of a huge flood that seemed to have been taking place at least once every other year in Singapore. They would prepare mostly porridge, salted vegetables, and sweet potatoes to tide them over till the flood subsided. Once they were done with cooking, they would spread the food over a couple of large bowls covered by plates of similar sizes and place them on top of cupboards or somewhere on the highest shelf in a cabinet beyond the reach of ferocious flood waters. These foods would then be consumed over the course of the long-drawn-out thunderstorm during which any form of cooking, no matter how basic, would be rendered infeasible. Should any household be caught in a hapless bind, for instance, if they failed to stock up enough food ingredients to last a couple of days—the invention of refrigerators was a decade away so overstocking was still unheard of—or if their matriarch had not been able to finish cooking prior to the storm, they could always avail themselves of other options to keep famishment at bay: munching bite-sized biscuits stored in airtight jars tucked away in almost every pantry in every house, eddying against the undertow to a neighbouring household to ask for food. In Lorong Limau, grudges, antipathies, issues of race and gender, however instructive, would normally dissolve in the wake of natural calamities such as floods and droughts. People would put aside their differences and conduct themselves as one united entity, except, of course, for the likes of Gau Pee who would rather die of starvation than approach Molly and her other mortal enemies for food. Similarly, she would not hesitate to turn away those she despised should they come begging for food at her very doorstep. In other words, esprit de corps just wasn't part of her vernacular.

'Girls, quick bring in the clothes!' Molly's mother voice boomed uncharacteristically across the stairwell. The walls between households were as porous as a sieve so one would often, by design or accident, pick up the details of other people's private lives: who was cursing who, who was having sex in the afternoon, who was having money problems—well, unsurprisingly, almost everyone for that matter—who was laughing, who was crying, who forgot to run an errand, who met who and who said what at the market.

'Anyone who has yet to shit today better shit right now!' Tin's mother bellowed, her voice bouncing off the walls and ceilings of her shack like an angry pinball. She had a point. Apart from ensuring food was being prepared, the other pertinent thing a matriarch would do was instruct members of her household to clear their bowels, since defecation inside the house would be inconceivable if not sanitarily repugnant during floods, as everything below crotch-level—chairs, mattresses, slippers, buckets—would be submerged in floodwaters.

Toilets of yore were not exactly blessed with dedicated flumes that would transport human waste by dint of gravity into some river or gorge let alone basic flushing systems, at least not in this country in the fifties. One would squat over a circular metallic container the size of a modern-day pizza and defecate within the confines of a makeshift shed located at the furthest end of any house, usually next to the open balcony or pantry. After that, they would cover the metallic container with a heavy sheet of zinc—weighed down by a couple of big granite stones in the event of a flood—to extenuate the fetor discharged into the orbit of the air inhaled by one's family members who would, ironically, at an early juncture in their lives, adapt themselves to the smell of human dross wafting around in their abode, sometimes even possessing the uncanny ability to decipher which odour stemmed from which family member. It was often said that there were only two types of smell an infant would first learn to detect in the house: the mother's natural body odour and the irrepressible whiff of shit.

Every day, a shit collector would show up at every household, haul the metallic container all the way to his truck and dump the contents into any of its thirty-six built-in, standard-size, drawer-like compartments, each occupying its own slot and removable using a handle. On days plagued by floods or general labour strikes, there would not be any shit collection, which meant people would be walking around the house with the necks of their shirts and samfus pulled up to their noses. Worse than that, worms could be crawling en masse out of the containers, all ready to party with abandon in the name of further waste decomposition.

'I'm going to poo poo now!' answered Kee Kee who would not be caught dead passing motion in the open fields covered with waters sometimes even up to the chest-level, especially if it continued to rain for ten to twelve hours without reprieve, not least submitting herself to a vile maelstrom of her own shit provoked by nature's remorseless toil. In most cases, people would find ways to thwart their biological calls as a result of this grave inconvenience. They would try not to eat much for the duration of the flood if they could help it. Drinking might also be kept to a minimum although, somehow, the notion of discharging urine in the open fields was commonly held as less disgusting than begriming the already murky waters with toxic, chunky pollutants of one's own making.

'Gan-ni-na! How many times must I tell you to clear your bowels first thing in the morning?' Tin's father yelled at Kee Kee who was making a dash to the toilet. 'What if your Ma hadn't reminded you? I guess you'd have infected this house with your shit once the flood hits us? Gan-ni-na!'

For all the concessions—waking up late, dodging housework—accorded to her by her mother, sisters, and brothers, Kee Kee could never elicit the same regard from her father. To be fair, the latter had always revelled in inventing insults for everyone in the family except Gau Pee whose financial contribution to the household continued to be valorized as significantly sizeable, derived primarily from the marketing of her home-made cookies as well as her services as a seamstress, a staple he knew better not to ruffle. So, one would never hear gan-ni-na and Gau Pee mentioned in the same breath.

As for Kee Kee, she had been inducted into his curse squad rather early on. It took place more than a decade ago during World War II when Singapore was invaded by the Japanese. In order to hide from the enemy, Tin's father with his family would hightail it out of the house into one of the air raid shelters in the open field—trenches dug way in advance, about ten feet deep, malodorous, full of ants—whenever the public siren came on, a loud droning sound to notify Singaporeans of yet another Japanese assault. At that time, Kee Kee was just an infant who had acquired the unfortunate habit of crying ex nihilo so Tin's father, visibly concerned that his entire family might be forced out of hiding and rounded up by the invaders due to the non-stop wailing of his youngest daughter and subsequently shot to death, took it upon himself to sacrifice her for the common good. Against a ferocious but eventually futile challenge mounted by Tin's mother, he hung Kee Kee by her wraparound garment on the hook of their front door instead of carrying her into the trench and putting everyone else's lives at risk. Naturally, Tin's mother accused him of being heartless, but he recriminated, saying she was not able to think straight; Kee Kee's siblings could only gasp in trepidation at the sight of their sister hung helplessly by the door and possibly getting killed but feared more for their own safety to beg their father to change his mind. Since then, Tin's father had grown to eye Kee Kee at a wary remove each time he recalled the Japanese occupation with unresolved venom, considering her a liability under the worst of circumstances and not hesitating to throw her to the lions once again if that was the only way to keep others in the family safe.

While Kee Kee was clearing her bowels, the voices of her fellow villagers trampled upon one another in a cacophony of anticipation and worry: 'Oh my, our crops are going to be destroyed again.' 'Where's your brother? Find him quick before the flood sets in!' 'Go hide the jewellery in a safe container!' 'Stack the chairs on the tables and leave the food there.' 'Come help mummy keep the clothes in a dry place.' 'Bring out the candles and matchsticks!'

The wind howled with terrifying ballast. Skies were grey and puffy with rain clouds. A torrential downpour seemed inevitable. When the rain finally came, it blasted down in massive slates, unremitting as an orgy of bullets in a battleground, making masturbatory mincemeat of nature and mankind. It was a scene of devastation. Tree branches cracked and fell on to the ground; a few splintered hulks here and there wrought barricades that failed to fortify the village against the furore of the waters; flumes emerged out of nowhere; piles of scrap, broken bicycles, and everything else either abandoned or in some relative state of disrepair drifted downstream to the main river coursing through the island of Singapore; crops were destroyed with no recourse; houses built of wood were decimated in a matter of minutes;

children who happened to be out playing catch in the fields or jumping over drains did not heed to the dangers of what was impending became casualties one way or another—the ones who managed to wade through waist-level waters to the safety of their homes merely suffered cuts, bruises, and ankle sprains while others not so fortunate found their limbs, ribs, or collarbones inadvertently crushed against buildings in the unfortunate event of being flushed around, helpless and disoriented, by copious currents and, it goes without saying, a few eventually died of hypothermia.

Within the first hour of rain, every foreseeable area in and outside Lorong Limau appeared to be flooded. The bleached-bone spaces between buildings were quickly replaced by a gurgling mass of water, eroding the very soil of open fields and assuming the colour of dirty brown. Homes were taken over by waist-level waters to the point where many people were found sitting on chairs stacked on top of tables. Some even braved the rain by climbing on to the rooftops of their not-too-long-ago sun-worn shacks to plant their butts and watch the flood ransack the milieu. Those who were more private by nature, preferring to close the front doors of their houses so that neighbours would not be able to see what was going on inside their living rooms and bedrooms, were now left with no choice but to open up their lives for scrutiny, since doors could no longer be shut due to the force of the waters although in times like these no one seriously had the zest to peek into the homes of others out of nosiness, as they were too preoccupied with their own flood management. Siblings who could hardly get along, like Tin and Gau Pee, found themselves spending time together, each in her own abyss,

held safe and tight by the other's silence, waiting patiently for
a lull in the downpour, improbable at least for the next eight
to nine hours based on past experience.

As far as Tin was concerned, the silence was like a balm.
Perched on a stool that had been placed on top of their family
dining table and watching the rest of her family members—
not including her older brother Ah Hock who was probably
stranded at his workplace—adrift in their own thoughts, she
felt light years away from the hurly-burly of the market where
she would normally be at this time of the morning had it not
been for the relentless rain. And despite the gushing noise of
water in the room, its gargling in the gutters that ran along the
whole length of their house, Tin was very much at peace, even
oddly uplifted. *Here's another rainstorm that might as well be weathered
in good cheer*, she said to herself. She then closed her eyes as
if she were about to start meditating. For no specific reason,
she dipped her wandering mind into the realm of fireflies and
broke out in a smile, mulling over the feasibility of nabbing a
few of those fireflies, storing them in a glass jar and using it to
set their living room aglow at night instead of relying on the
prevalent sources of light such as kerosene lamps and candles.

Around her, nobody was in the mood to chat—not
that she craved it, certainly not at all. Tin's mother seemed
to be surveying her surrounding with an air of languid
detachment and fatigue, having fervently spent the last hour
cooking a day's worth of food and packing all their clothes in
waterproof rubberized bags which her oldest daughter Pao
had donated to her instead of throwing them away; Gau Pee
appeared distant, probably mentally scheming against the
likes of Molly or hatching a plan to take over the running

of Lorong Limau from Jude Vincent one day; Kee Kee was obviously bored, sitting atop a high chair and watching the water underneath her feet with the same fascination one would accord to watching milk sour; Bok Koon, Tin's younger school-going brother, seemed wrapped up in his own bubble of wonderment having just witnessed the unfolding of an outcome so affecting and overwhelming that it might call other realities into doubt—he and Kee Kee were both too young to recall the ravages of World War II, unlike their older siblings, so a flood would invariably be their ne plus ultra of upheavals experienced while growing up; most uncharacteristically quiet though was Tin's father whose usual largess of stinging gan-ni-nas appeared to be in heavy deficit after his last curse had been directed at Kee Kee before the latter scurried off to defecate prior to the thunderstorm.

The quiet's really soothing, Tin mused. No sooner had she ushered in her contentment than she found the reason behind it smashed into smithereens.

'Ouch!' Kee Kee yelped, accidentally falling from her high chair into the water and knocking her knees against the concrete floor of the living room.

Gau Pee let loose a sinister laugh, shrill and condescending, a manifestation of schadenfreude that she would gladly deliver merely to seize the last straw of dignity from whoever was in trouble or experiencing misfortune; Tin's mother rushed to Kee Kee's side to find out if her daughter was badly hurt—a light bruise was all she had to worry about although in the mind of Kee Kee, a self-perpetuating aristocratic futurist at odds with her present living conditions, a lifetime sooner than her projected ideal, it was more than a discounted injury, by far the most savage humiliation ever to have encumbered her fragile, royal soul.

'This can't be happening. I'm not supposed to suffer any more than this flood has already inflicted on me. No, this isn't fair,' Kee Kee cried out.

'Gan-ni-na, you'd better shut up! Why must you always be the one getting all of us worked up for nothing?' Tin's father yelled at her.

'Take it easy, I'm handling it,' Tin's mother said, directing her comment at everyone in the room instead of just her husband so that it would not be seen as a riposte that might further compound his anger. Grabbing Kee Kee by her upper arm, she yanked her up, whispered something into her ears and patted her head. Before long, both were back in their seats, clothes soaking wet. The prior quiet of the house was now thickened by the brooding characters in it, their restlessness and rustling and unusually deep breaths.

A paragon of sexual vigour—that was how Ah Hock saw himself. So did the women of the Glorious Hole Brothel. At first it was just hearsay based on one woman's account. Gradually, a few others who'd had the chance to be with him started saying the same thing, about how he could sustain a forward momentum following his initial orgasm, showing no hint of a slowdown let alone gradual exhaustion, and soon enough the heathen became the converted as more and more prostitutes got in line to have a taste of Ah Hock.

This morning he could be found in the brothel doing what he did best, since not much else was happening at the Central Post Office, his workplace. For certain, there was not going to be any delivery of letters, what with the thunderstorm so he decided to visit the brothel like he occasionally would in the evening after work, a salubrious outing—in his mind, at least—that would put the harsh realities of life behind him even if it was only meant to be temporary.

Lying down on his back, stripped to his underwear with a couple of women around him in a similar state of undress, he inhaled the opium vapour with steadfastness via a smoking pipe, started rambling on about his childhood, how he would bully the other boys into giving him their marbles and cards, punctuating his sentences from time to time with a kind of dreamy psychedelic laughter. The women seemed to be having a good time soaking in his prattle as they caressed his chest and arms in a slow deliberate fashion, waiting patiently for him to lead them down the Yellow Brick Road.

The Glorious Hole Brothel was set up by the infamous Looi family which also happened to sire other illegal businesses such as gambling dens and money laundering services. With several acres of land and a shipping business empire under its belt, the Looi clan certainly had the financial arsenal to outgun authorities that had managed to shut down a couple of their prohibited operations in the past only to witness with wide-eyed resignation the blooming of twice the number of similar entities within weeks of their raids and cessations.

It was precisely the likes of Ah Hock and other randy characters who had first invoked the opportunist in Mr Looi, the greybeard of the clan. Every so often, he would encounter men, specifically a large proportion of the working class— singles as well as married ones in the absence of their wives, of course—gathered together to talk about sex, about how belabouring and inviable it was for them to seek women for the sake of pleasure and how unfair that only the rich could afford to do so with specially-hired pimps. At that point, he was able to envision quick and easy profitability, knowing lasciviousness could be exploited at an affordable price tag with a ready pool of cheap women for hire and that his business could very well provide a refuge for both the sexually modest and the prurient. Hence, the birth of the Glorious Hole Brothel. In the end, Mr Looi not only managed to coax the common man out of his sexual confines but also tap into the collective libidos of thousands of British soldiers stationed in post-war Singapore during that period in time.

While there was no doubt that Ah Hock belonged to the prurient group, it was not just sex he was pursuing that morning in the brothel. He reckoned it would be safer, drier, and more comfortable to sit out the storm here—windows firmly shut, doors concrete enough to withstand any water pressure—as opposed to the small, wretched unit of a shack in which he had been living with his parents and siblings. Besides, he also reckoned it would not hurt to get high on opium and plow a few ladies along the way.

Spot-on was Ah Hock's assessment of the brothel as a fortress against thunderstorms and floods. Situated just beyond the periphery of Lorong Limau, it was a two-storey building with grey walls and squarish red windows fronted by Tembusu trees, one of the safest and most reliable asylums in the neighbourhood to withstand the elements of nature. No doubt some water would seep into the ground floor of the building despite its air-tight doors and windows not to mention a sufficient supply of sandbags at its disposal, but overall, the place would still remain relatively dry and snug.

To the residents of Lorong Limau and other neighbouring villages, it was common knowledge that nothing honourable would ever take place inside the compound of the brothel and many would cast supercilious glances at the building whenever they happened to walk past it; some would simply prefer not to acknowledge its presence or talk about it especially with young children around. Even teenagers, having caught wind of its sordid reputation, were not above behaving the same way as their parents despite being more liberal-minded than people from other age groups. To the uninitiated or unfamiliar, the place was merely a hotel; in fact, the neon sign clearly read 'Glorious Hole Hotel'. Of course, one did not have to receive a formal education to fathom the irony of its name. To the police, bringing the corrupted wealthy Looi clan to justice would remain their onus although several high-level raids on the brothel in the last few years had rendered nothing more than a bunch of pretty women sitting around having tea and waiting to welcome guests to their hotel (the police had no knowledge of an underground escape route from the building where patrons could leave in a jiffy and, more importantly, take cover without getting arrested).

Its ground floor comprised a rather airy reception area with an adjoining courtyard, a fully equipped kitchen, a common relaxation room where guests could mingle and discuss their post-coital experience, and a no-entry staff room belonging to the matron, the second wife of the Looi household and reportedly Mr Looi's favourite among his four wives, who used it largely for storing her own possessions, namely jewellery and clothes, together with cigarettes and opium leaves reserved strictly for guests. On the second floor, there were ten chambers of varying sizes and furnishings—the most expensive came with an imposing bed, a wardrobe, an inlaid table, upholstered chairs, and an exquisite well-stocked bathroom and the cheapest one was currently being occupied by Ah Hock.

The matron and her entourage of whores were familiar with every client's background and spending capability. They were also intimately aware of their fetishes and so-called hot buttons. In essence, what was often discussed and shared among the prostitutes in private, chaired by the matron—penis size, performance hang-up, and sexual prowess of clients—was primarily meant to serve the brothel's overall mission: create a unique experience for every customer. For instance, if a repeat client was known to take an exceedingly long time to climax, the girls in his company would slip on patience like a second skin; if he enjoyed having his nipples gnawed at, they would act accordingly with his preferred dosage and intensity. The possession of such valuable insight would lead to a high regard for the brothel among its clients and ultimately keep them coming back for more.

In Ah Hock's case, he was not only perceived as a satyr but also a connoisseur of the female anatomy, especially the backside. To that end, the matron knew exactly what kind of derrières would turn him on. For starters, there was nothing he enjoyed more than staring at the outline of a pair of cheeks squeezed tightly underneath a dress or samfu. He had spent many a year since attaining puberty examining as well as relishing this specific body part, its tautness and shape, and how it could further be enshrined in a pair of sexy-looking panties. At times, the mere sight of it, especially if the woman was buxom and vivacious, would cause him to become loaded between his legs in a heartbeat. And speaking of cocks, he certainly had one that Michelangelo would have swooned to sketch which more or less explained his popularity with the whores that ruled the brothel. Every time he would pay them a visit, they would tremble in wild anticipation, hoping to be picked for one of his orgies involving four to five women at any one time. Needless to say, these activities cost money; so did the consumption of opium for which Ah Hock had a random craving although nowhere close to an addiction. Hence, with his penchant for drinking, gambling, frequenting whores and hollering to the moon about the best backsides he had seen in Singapore each time he was high on opium, not only had he lied to his parents about his take-home pay, thereby contributing nothing to the household financially speaking ('I can't even make enough money to support myself let alone this family') but he had also, by way of shamelessly dialling up the sympathy factor with a thrawn expression, managed to siphon a few dollars here and there from his mother who would then make more tarts and sew more clothes while blaming herself for not being able to provide a conducive home with enough money and comfort for her older son to study well—even though Ah Hock had never bothered to swot and had ultimately dropped out of school—thus causing him to lose out on the better prospects in life. Tin's mother had since vowed not to repeat history with Bok Koon, trying her darn best to make her younger one complete his education at least up till O-level.

'Bring me more leaves,' Ah Hock instructed the three prostitutes in the room, no larger than the pantry at his workplace, rather spartan except for a mirror, a pounder, and a pipe (both accessories for the use of opium) and an elevated wooden platform on which they were all resting their loins. The room had only one ill-fitting window looking out into a garden with more weeds than grass, beholding which at the moment one just could not differentiate between the two types of plants given the ongoing rain and flooding. He spoke eagerly and with an energy that was almost importunate so much so that one of the women—a young girl, slim, flat-chested, barely in her late teens—hastily put on her clothes and left the room to fetch what Ah Hock had requested.

'Come on, can't I have some form of entertainment while waiting?' he pleaded, rapping the surface of the wooden platform with his knuckles.

The other two women—easily a decade older than the one who had just left the room—began twirling in front of him much to his delight, their naked breasts resiling back and forth as they caressed each other and pouted seductively. He clapped his hands in approval and shouted 'more' over and over. Inhaling yet another plume of vapour from the opium pipe, he tilted his head and summoned the ladies to stop dancing and give him a blow job. As they gathered around his prized behemoth and fed on it with arrhythmic swish, he moaned in a falsetto that had seldom seen the light of day in his normal parlance as though a chance scatter of stars had indeed resolved into a constellation for mankind. 'More,' he squeaked.

The third woman who had earlier left the room came back within minutes clutching a bunch of opium leaves in her palm. She placed the leaves in the pounder and started pounding away. Once that was done, she doffed her samfu and brought the pounder with the leaves in it to Ah Hock, her supple, girlish mouth poised in an expression of eager servility. Dismissing the oral services of her other two comrades with the flat of his hand, Ah Hock closed his eyes and sniffed at the leaves for a while. A smile broke out on his assessment.

'This one's imported for sure,' he uttered exuberantly, his erection still intact. As the saying goes, once you've been smoking opium for quite some time, you can identify a good harvest blindfolded.

All three women cooed in unison. The youngest one waltzed back to where she had left her samfu on the concrete floor, retrieved a matchbox from one of its pockets and passed it to Ah Hock.

'You can light it up, sir!' she said, sounding as if she had spent time in a prison cell and was about to be released on good behaviour.

Ah Hock struck a match, brought the flame near the open mouth of the opium pipe where the pounded leaves had been consolidated and slowly inhaled the first cloud that emerged. The women took turns to smoke thereafter, an occupational ritual to which many of these prostitutes were wont. Some did it to numb their professional anxiety, as they would not be able to tell if a new client would turn out to be abusive or dangerously kinky, some to distil the pain inflicted by repeat clients who were in fact abusive—many of whom came from wealthy households and did not have to work a day in their lives—into piecemeal bearable thresholds, others to simply nullify the shame of being a prostitute, not least during the period of sexual engagement.

'All right, let me test you all,' he said in a playful, moony tone, sitting on the platform, back against the wall, chest and arms being caressed by the women. 'Whoever can answer my question correctly will get an extra twenty cents from me. Yes? Are you all ready?'

They bolted upright, showing him the eager beavers they could transform themselves into at the snap of a finger despite the out-of-body hallucinatory effect of opium.

'Listen carefully then. What kind of illness can be cured by opium?' he asked, laughing mid-question, as his last inhalation seemed to have rubbed off on him rather strongly.

'I know, I know!' exclaimed one of the twenty-somethings, the one who had more meat around her hips. 'Opium can cure pain. Yes?'

'You stupid woman! Opium can't do that, it can only numb the pain for a while,' he shouted. 'And by the way, pain is not an illness.' He laughed again as if he had just cracked a joke that tickled him even as it was being told. But since everyone else was high, it did not matter whether his laughter was at odds with what he was saying. It also did not matter that it was terribly fuggy inside the room due to the shut window and the lack of ventilation. The rain was lashing with gusto at the exterior of the building; the storm appeared unappeased.

'Come on, it's really a no-brainer. Anyone?' he persisted with a twinkle in his eye. Without a doubt, the women loved the way he twinkled. They caressed him with increased intensity and planted kisses all over his body. Ah Hock was also handsome, the brute kind of handsome. He had piercing eyes, angular cheeks, and rather small ears; he was neither skinny nor fat, just blessed with a strapping physique like his father when the latter had been his age; also like his father, he was more of a lout. But he tended to be gentle during sex, perhaps aware that not every woman was born to engulf his ginormous wiener—rock-solid even after all this time without any oral assistance—nor built anatomically to dovetail into it. It also helped that the figure he cut was one of perfect composure, putting any prostitute at ease especially if she were to have pre-performance anxiety.

'Oh, I think I know,' said the youngest of the trio. 'It's tuberculosis!'

'Finally!' he said, slurring the word, laughing even louder than the sound of thunder outside. He inhaled the vapour, this time in one sturdy, unbroken swoop. It seemed to have burrowed so deeply into his otherworldliness and his inertia that he found himself recapitulating what he thought of the butts around him ('I can just eat your arses all day') not for their fleshiness, though they were fleshy indeed except for the one belonging to the youngest, but for precipitating his fetish, a sole distraction from the penury he so despised and had to endure throughout his life thus far. If Tin's mother could see him now—loafing away, prostitutes by his side, high on opium, she would have had a conniption.

'All right ladies, it's showtime!' he said, struggling to stand up, knees wobbling, arms propped up with the help of the three women together. 'Now I'm really going to eat your arses!' Barely a few seconds on his feet, Ah Hock collapsed on the wooden platform.

'It's already three o'clock and Ah Hock's still not back. I just hope he's keeping himself safe and dry,' Tin's mother said to no one in particular. Propped by a chair on the table, she hauled herself up to retrieve the food—porridge and bean sprouts—that had been cooked prior to the thunderstorm and placed on top of the cupboard in the living room; she then portioned the food into a few bowls, one for each person: her husband, herself and her four children present. She figured they must be hungry by now, not having eaten anything since the onset of the flood six hours ago for fear of defecating in the name of public comity. 'No food, no shit,' Tin's father would iterate to quell any hunger pangs.

'He's obviously trapped in the post office like we are in the house right now,' Gau Pee said. 'Besides, you don't expect him to cycle home in this weather, do you?'

'I just hope he's safe, that's all,' Tin's mother murmured.

The water level had since subsided, though not substantially enough to precipitate the resumption of normal life. Many villagers were still trying to keep dry by perching themselves on higher ground and kill time by chatting with family members, throat willing, or catching a few winks at their own peril. The storm was still unrelenting with heavy rain pelting down; the sky was the same monotonous grey.

Every member of Tin's family appeared to be hunched over his or her bowl and busy tucking into the porridge except Kee Kee who simply looked at it and whined, 'Huh, porridge again? Why can't we have something different to cheer us up in times like this? I mean aren't we sick of eating the same stuff day-in day-out?'

'Gan-ni-na, one more word from you and I'll crack your head like an egg!' Tin's father issued a stern warning to his youngest daughter who immediately consumed her food in begrudging silence.

'There are biscuits and sweet potatoes in the pantry if we happen to run out of porridge by day's end,' Tin's mother interjected, knowing the responsibility of preparing enough food to last through the storm would always sit squarely on her shoulders. Her life, after all, had been an endless round of cooking for her family and making all sorts of *kuey kuey*s for sale.

'I wonder if Ah Hock has already had something to eat. He must be hungry by now,' Tin's mother sighed. Like most mothers of that era, her children only really came into focus when in isolation or missing in action due in part to the number of children competing for her attention at any one time more than she could punctiliously manage, and in part to a large chunk of her time being taken up by household chores and the selling of kuey kueys. Together they were an unwieldy flock, singly they managed to seize her notice.

'Would you want me to keep part of my porridge for him? As it is, I'm not particularly hungry,' Tin said, facing her mum and awaiting her silent nod of the head.

'Oh, for God's sake, don't try to act like you're some sort of good Samaritan,' said Gau Pee, brushing aside Tin's sincerity in an offhand manner that she would often employ while debunking the existence of ghosts ('Only stupid people will believe in something as ridiculous as ghosts.')

'It's all right. I've reserved some food for him in the pantry,' said Tin's mother who cautiously sidestepped her favourite daughter's innuendo so as not to provoke her temper. 'I think it would be best that we fill our own stomachs to the brim, as the storm may last for another few hours.'

'Time to eat!' They could hear Molly's mother gathering her children and apportioning loaves of bread among them

('Let's not eat your full share of bread so we will have enough if the flood lasts longer than expected.') The walls between their houses were paper-thin so it was pretty common for one to overhear such things. In any case, the residents of Lorong Limau could not really be bothered by the lack of privacy; many recognized it as the consequence of poverty. They knew they would be living in homes with more soundproof walls and better sanitation if they had a lot of money to begin with. But people like Tin who prized privacy more than most things in life would often reduce their voices to a whisper in the discussion of matters they considered best left unheard by eavesdroppers.

'Ma, would you then mind if I were to share some of my porridge with Molly?' Tin asked her mother. 'I think there may not be enough bread to go around in her family.'

'Sure,' Tin's mother replied although there was something unsure about the way she said she was sure which made Tin think maybe she was not completely agreeable to the idea of giving away food to someone else. After all, her own family might not even have a quantity sufficient to see them though nightfall, biscuits and sweet potatoes in the pantry notwithstanding, so neither Tin nor anyone could fault her for thinking along the line of self-preservation (family-first to be accurate) if that was truly the case.

'Not so fast!' Gau Pee raised her voice. 'Who says we are in a position to share food with others? What gives you the right to make this unilateral decision?' She was targeting her spite at her younger sister, certainly not at her mother.

'Gau Pee, why don't we—' Tin's mother attempted to say something before her daughter jumped right back into the dialogue.

'This is not fair, Ma. You know we all work so hard just to make ends meet. I mean right now we don't even know whether we will have enough money to go marketing in the next few days,' Gau Pee put across her argument grimly.

'Gan-ni-na, what's all this *kau-pei-kau-bu*?' Tin's father fired off, calling it a verbal chaos. 'The storm is already making me crankier than ever. Can't all of you just keep quiet and eat your porridge?'

Nobody stirred. They ate in silence and relinquished the subject matter as quickly as it had found its footing a few minutes ago. After this, the hours continued to pass in a blur of rain-droned sameness.

Through a kaleidoscope of dust, like particles trapped between eyelashes, he could barely make out a patch of grey sky with a faint beam of sunlight cutting across his line of vision. He tried to open his eyes fully, but his eyelids felt heavy. His clothes were soaking wet, leaving his skin pimpled and teeth chattering. Leaning against the exterior wall of what appeared to be a decrepit bullet-scarred building, he found most parts of his lower body covered in sludge as the rain had turned everything into a kind of glutinous grit. The smell around him was disgustingly rank; he felt like throwing up. The last thing, he recalled, buzzing in his head was some kind of argument: 'He's dead, I think he's dead, we'd better throw him into the river, we can't call the police, no doctor too.' For sure, he did not know where he was. The whole place looked desolate; behind him, against which he was leaning, was the dilapidated building (that, unbeknownst to him at that moment, would lead to the sewers), to his right an expanse of ankle-deep feculent water, and further down his left another vacant derelict two-storey building, probably a shophouse not too long ago whose business might have been decimated by a changing tide of commerce. *Oh god, what's the smell again?* He tried barfing but to no avail.

As if by an edict of the gods, the rain had stopped, the wind eased. In fact, the storm had softened following almost nine continuous hours of downpour. It was early evening. After the rain, the sun seemed chastened and tentative, and had the first frisson of post-monsoon in it. The flood had also subsided with the water level reduced to a shoal.

Every memory of his seemed vague, at best jam-packed with curdled permutations borrowed from his subconscious. A last gust of opium. Darkness fell, swift and unyielding. A rebellious murmuring from the three women who insisted Ah Hock was either wasted or dead ('I've checked . . . he's no longer breathing,' said one. 'Could he have just fainted?' asked another). The voice of the matron. Panic mode. Other than that, everything else was completely blotted out.

For certain, he recalled nothing about the matron insisting that she simply was not going to involve the police, as they would gladly take this opportunity to shut down the bordello for good. Worse, they may even use it as an excuse to go after all the other illegal businesses run by the Looi clan on which they had been keeping tabs for the longest time. Neither could she approach a doctor to confirm if Ah Hock was truly dead for fear the doctor might start asking questions that she was not prepared to answer. Quickly, she held his wrist to verify whether he still had a pulse; she detected none. Almost sure he was dead, the matron together with her three employees started dressing Ah Hock with the clothes he had discarded on the floor when he was busy cooing at the ladies to get naked with him early on. The hardest part of the exercise, they discovered, was squeezing his (gasp!) half-erected joystick into his pants. Even though they reckoned he might already be dead, they couldn't bear to not be gentle with his distended member, to so much as fracture one of its veins, thinking it would be an unpardonable crime, graver than the idea of dumping his body into a river. One would have thought Ah Hock's sudden collapse should have completely taken the wind out of his bulge, but it did not. 'A real man,' the women concurred among themselves.

Then came the critical decision: how to dispose of the body in the most humanitarian manner without leaving incriminating evidence at the same time although, to be honest, they were not unduly worried about the evidence part knowing the local police were mostly not up to snuff. It was no secret the police had proven themselves time and again to be able to only handle cases that were not anything baroque or complicated in nature like giving chase to someone who had just stolen an item from a vendor and resolving a fight between two hooligans on the street. Other than that, homicide or murder would seem a case as Sisyphean as getting them to rid the world of mosquitoes and ants.

The bigger consideration then would be the humanitarian part. There was no denying how much they adored Ah Hock. He had never forfeited his payments nor had he ever manhandled the ladies; he was not out-of-shape or unremittingly ugly unlike the usual Tans, Lims, Lees, and Kohs frequenting Glorious Hole nor had he ever fallen short of public decorum during the times he had spent in the joint.

'I think we should deliver his corpse back to his family after the storm and tell them we'd found him lying dead in the gutters near our brothel'; 'No, let's give him a proper send-off by letting his body float down the river as our ancestors had done so with their loved ones from time immemorial'; 'Better yet, we'll send his body up north to Malaya and have him buried there.' The argument had gone on long enough, the matron decided. She knew exactly what she had to do. 'Cover him with a bed sheet from head to toe,' she instructed the three women.

After the rain had ceased and floodwaters receded, the matron got her personal driver and the three ladies to carry Ah Hock to her car through the backdoor of Glorious Hole, a narrow driveway adjacent to a piece of parched land where only stray dogs were wont to lurk around. Very few people would want to take the route past that area, as they feared getting bitten by these dogs and thereby hurtling themselves precipitously into the fatal world of rabies. With Ah Hock in the trunk, they drove about ten miles towards the west and then deposited his body near the sewers, basically a no man's land.

Obviously, he remembered none of that. He did not know how he ended up where he was. Struggling to stand up, he let out a chorus of moans that would have done credit to a hippopotamus in labour. His blood must have been chilled by the rain and surrounding waters during his period of inertia so much so that when he attempted to move, it stung him to the core. He rested for a while more, trying to decipher his whereabouts. He saw a labyrinth of huge pipes connected possibly to the ground below which seemed to be spouting water continuously into the landscape, giving rise to a pool of filthy water on his right side which he had noticed earlier. And then a shadow of alarm passed over his face. The stench from the sewers had steadily grown forbidding in proportion to his surge in clarity. He was worried he might faint again if he did not try to escape from the fetor.

By far though, his bigger worry was figuring out what to tell his parents once he got home assuming he could find his way back considering his sense of direction must have been snarled up by the cold and the lingering effects of whatever had taken place in the brothel during the period he suspected he might have been unconscious. Against all odds, he eventually got on his feet. He also felt terribly hungry, suddenly reminiscing about the smell of sweet potatoes wafting through the living room of his house and imagining eating the tarts made (for sale) by his mother and sisters, crispy and buttery, and also wolfing down rice dumplings they would make once a year during the Spring Festival. Ah Hock's thoughts soon strayed to the warmth of his bed, a mattress actually, to dreams full of beautiful women, their bums and the swelling of breasts beneath their dresses all of which held loaded power to the point of triggering a mini marshland in his already soaked trousers.

In his mind, he was not above admitting that he might have overdosed on opium; incidentally, he was not even angry with the ladies from Glorious Hole for abandoning him if he were to believe the puzzle he had pieced together in the past few minutes—they must have panicked and decided to leave him near some deserted sewers so that they would be free of any monkey on their back, the police that is. If anything, he knew he had only himself to blame. In the presence of his family, he would of course all but exculpate himself from every infraction—the brothel, the opium, the wasted money—and deftly fabricate a story of how he avoided the storm by remaining in the post office and how he accidentally cycled over a concrete slab and fell while making his way home, hence the soiled clothes and shoes, in order to milk everyone's sympathy, particularly his mother's, and to continue asking her for money from time to time to feed his voluptuous yearnings.

But it did not cross his mind that he would never see his mother again. While trudging for what seemed like the longest time he had ever spent searching for a thoroughfare with the intent of boarding a bus or better yet, catching a ride from a kind soul, he fell into a muddy hole, as deep as a well, and crashed his head against a boulder, a swift death that offered not a minute more to either cry for help or salivate over some imaginary female butt oscillating in his head.

Part II

Part II

Chapter Seven

The police were all over the place. A tip-off by the captain of the American ship had brought them to the port and set forth one of the most dramatic raids ever. The captain was a religious man and certainly would not be caught dead allowing his men to shag prostitutes on the ship itself, not on his watch. Apparently, one of his deckhands had earlier informed him that a group of 'self-made women' would be paying the sailors a visit once the ship was docked for replenishments and maintenance. It was too short a time— one to two hours at most to load and unload the cargoes—for the sailors to hit town and get laid yet too long for them to sit around and pretend they were nonchalant about their sexual urges having been out at sea without any female company for several months on end, so one of them took the initiative to telegraph in advance his buddy from Singapore, a well-known pimp, to arrange for a select group of women, for sure the best-looking ones in the pimp's circle, to come on board and restore their inalienable right to exist below the waist for as long as the ship was to remain docked.

Headed by Jim Vincent, the only child of Jude Vincent, who was the appointed head of Lorong Limau, the police made a forced entry into the private lounge in the bilge area. There, they rounded up twenty-five men and eight women, all butt-naked obviously, indulging themselves in what appeared to be an orgy. The police apprehended the women but let the sailors off the hook with a stern warning, an agreement negotiated between the captain and Jim Vincent vis-à-vis the tip-off.

'Urgh . . . can I just take a few more minutes to finish what I started?' pleaded one of the sailors who adamantly refused to withdraw his instrument from the rear of the woman he was shagging despite the police barging into the lounge, blowing their whistles and asking everyone to immediately halt what they were doing. When Jim Vincent threatened to slice off what little he suspected was down there (Jim was right—it was merely a pinprick of flesh upon its withdrawal from her docking station), the sailor backed down instantly, albeit with agitated reluctance. In sharp contrast, the rest of his comrades were seen scrambling for their clothes, once the police had stormed into the room, enmeshed in multiple heaps of clothing piled up helter-skelter on the floor. 'Damn it', 'shit', 'oh god', 'no way', the air was weighed down with shouts of fear, anger, and agony.

If you think the women would be the first to gasp and shriek in arrant humiliation, you could not be more wrong. Emanating more *froideur* than the Alaskan ice masses through which the ship had navigated during a part of its journey, there was hardly a flicker of panic in their collective expression as they remained reclined on the lounge sofa with legs spread out or bent over a tabletop or kneeling down on the floor, suddenly without anything firm to hold on to. In fact, they were not the least bashful about their own nudity compared to the men who, out of desperation to hide their penises from view, struggled to get into their clothes and tumbled over one another when they each tried to squeeze both feet into one trouser leg by accident. The women simply took their time to sort out their clothes and only started to get dressed when Jim Vincent vehemently told them to do so without further delay.

'Sir, I suspect there's one more group above this deck. Would you like to check it out?' said Jim Vincent's trusted second-in-command, Mohammed Noor.

'How do you know?' Jim Vincent queried.

'One deckhand told me so,' Mohammed Noor replied. In fact, it was the same deckhand who had earlier informed his captain about the visit by the prostitutes. Like the captain, the deckhand also professed to be a religious man, proudly telling Mohammed Noor at one point that he would rather commit suicide than live with the sin of carnality outside marriage, although he had clearly elided two facts: he had never been married, and he enjoyed stealing glances at fellow sailors whenever they were in the showers. He had also failed to mention how much at odds he often felt in their company, especially when they started to talk smutty and made him begrudgingly indulge their obsession with tits and cunts. He hated every bit of it.

'I lost my husband to a devil,' Mona Sanchez would often tell her group of friends whose count had since thinned to an impervious few after she had become a lady of the night having failed to secure a job in almost every line of trade no matter how hard she persisted. It all started when her husband passed away. She was forced to sell their bungalow to pay off his outstanding business loan and other debts with just enough leftover money to put down a deposit for renting a shack in Lorong Limau. With zero income and practically no financial assistance from family and relatives—her parents had since passed away and she did not have any siblings—Mona had to find a job to support her visually-impaired mother-in-law and her two teenage sons (the older one, an eighteen-year-old, attending university; the younger one, a sixteen-year-old, still in secondary school). She did not even have the luxury to grieve the passing of her husband. As soon as his funeral was over, Mona started looking frantically for a job. But no one seemed to want to take a chance on her. She was told she was too ladylike to handle menial tasks ('You're born to break bowls, not carry or wash them,' said a fish-ball noodle vendor), too clueless about cooking or baking which could have earned her a living no matter how measly, too educated for her own good (she had learnt some English in her younger days but clerical work was strictly an all-men's territory) and too unskilled for jobs like housekeeping and sewing of uniforms, prevalent in the British army barracks set up in Singapore after World War II prior to the country's independence.

In her darkest moments, she blamed her husband for everything. If he had not died, she would still be enjoying a life of comfort—a band of servants preparing meals and running household chores for her family, a lot of money and time to dress up and look pretty, a big house with an even bigger adjoining garden. Now she was penniless and had to find means to feed herself and three other dependents, living in a tiny, cramped house in one of the poorest villages ever; she also realized a little too late that all along she had been mixing with fair-weather friends, as none of them had even bothered to listen to her sob story let alone help her out financially after her husband's demise. *Shit you*, she would sometimes quietly curse him before crying herself to sleep at night.

At first, she made no mental conjugation between a seemingly harmless comment uttered by her husband at the cemetery where they had paid their last respects to his grandmother and the fact that he was robbed of his life without warning until much later when she started to connect the dots. He had said, 'I love it here for the air is so crisp,' and he had died of a sudden heart attack the following day. 'The devil had claimed his life,' she would lament.

According to folklore, it was believed that visitors to a cemetery would often stuff a blade of grass into their mouths so as to remind themselves to not say a word for fear of uttering something that the spirits lurking around could use against them, sort of a superstitious interdiction against verbalizing anything deemed offensive to the dead. She wished she had regarded this folklore more seriously, as she could have forewarned her husband, and he might still have been alive right now. *Why didn't I? How could I have ignored something as ominous as this? No, I'm not to be blamed . . . he's the one who's responsible for his own tragedy. After all, he must have heard far too many times from his high-society friends stories of people who'd passed away under the most mysterious circumstances just because they unwittingly said something at the cemetery—how a man, after catching a glimpse of a woman's photo on her gravestone and extolling her beauty, had hanged himself the following day leaving a suicide note that said, 'He had no choice but to succumb to the will of beauty,' and how another man who had, for no reason at all, decided to gorge himself with food till he died from overeating, having jokingly mentioned to the person next to him at the cemetery the day before that he would want a bigger burial space when his time on earth was eventually up and that he would never settle for a teeny weeny tombstone like the one in front of him at that point in time.*

Mona was mad at her husband. But she was even more furious with herself for not being able to clinch even the simplest of jobs. In no time, though, her luck experienced a turnaround when she ran into a childhood friend one desultory afternoon, another single mother who had initially faced difficulty finding a job after her own husband's passing but gladly ended up as a prostitute. After listening to Mona's sob story, this friend tried to convince her that prostitution, illegality and stigmatization notwithstanding, would in fact enable her to make a reasonably secure living, citing herself as an example; she had managed to raise her children all these years on her own, not that anyone would help her either, since she had lost all her friends and relatives in the course of spreading her legs open any time, anywhere.

During their little chat, Mona's friend said to her: 'You need to ask yourself, do you care more about shame or survival?' The truth was she cared equally about both. Did she have the means to rule out prostitution as a livelihood option? If not, what would her children and mother-in-law think of her? What would her friends think of her? Most important of all, what would she think of herself? That she had lost her wealth and moved to Lorong Limau was already a hard pill to swallow although she felt there was nothing shameful about being poor or deracinated. Prostitution, on the other hand, stood for everything that was ignominious. Ignominiousness sure had deep pockets, even deeper than identity itself. It could ruin your life and that of others you loved. It could bore its way in and expose you for who you would really turn into till you would have nothing to show for yourself and could not stand a thing about your own existence. And you would make up for it by blaming everyone else for resorting to one-sided arguments and inflammatory language to impugn prostitution as a means to all but survive.

No way was she going to stoop lower than she already had—what with an abrupt, disconcerting change in lifestyle— she decided, so she went on searching for that elusive job only to be rejected a hundred times over. In the face of haplessness, she began to cherish no illusion of work for herself, a dire prospect which meant no money, not even a rented shack in Lorong Limau, no future whatsoever. It would thus ill become her to remain resistant to the option of making a living as a prostitute, if not for herself then certainly for the sake of her two sons and her blind mother-in-law who had shown her nothing but kindness and care since the day she married her son and moved into their bungalow. She needed to make sure she could at least maintain a roof over their heads and feed them on a daily basis because the last thing she would want was for her sons to drop out of school and take up menial work in order to chip in financially. Sure, her children would not approve of her line of work should they eventually find out but she was confident of winning them over as long as she could explain that money had to come from some place, that she earned it the hard way, that there was no longer a fat savings account into which they could tap as they had in the past. But for now, she would just tell them she was a clerk working in some office. *Perfidy for a good cause*, she thought.

The funny thing was that Mona Sanchez, a thirty-five-year-old of Eurasian descent, did not exactly have a full grasp of her own beauty until she became a prostitute. As a child, she would often hear her mother's friends compliment her mum on how lucky she was to have such a beautiful daughter with a marmoreal complexion and alluring hazel eyes. 'You're such a pretty girl. A real beauty. That perfect face.' But she hardly dwelled on their superlatives not because she did not believe them but rather she had her mind on other things like chasing butterflies on the field, playing a game of catch with her fellow neighbours, and laughing silly at themselves. Later on, over a stretch of years, she was more concerned about survival than looking pretty what with the war and the Japanese occupation of Singapore.

By the time she turned sixteen, matchmakers would seek out her mother to propose a surefire catch for her, much like starry-eyed teenagers huddling round their movie idol for an autograph. Rumour had it that there were dozens of men lining up to become her husband, each as rich, handsome, and of reputable upbringing as the other but she simply resisted succumbing to these pre-connubial genuflections, reckoning men in general would find any decent-looking woman like herself irresistibly attractive as long as they were short of possessing her sexually. The day she got married, she wowed everyone at her wedding ceremony. Extolments ranging from 'the most beautiful bride ever' to 'God's wondrous gift to man' echoed profusely in the church where she and her husband tied the knot. As a wife, the unstinting adoration which continued to shadow her—from time to time her husband would tease her about how exceptionally captivating she looked and how lucky he was to be married to her—seemed not to have registered deep enough in her consciousness to make her fully appreciative of her assets, since she thought her husband had always been playfully glib by nature and it would be foolish of her to take his raillery to heart.

However, when she started picking up men to make money, it did not take her long to be convinced that she owned a trump card over and above the rest of her competition based solely on appearance. Soon, it became a game changer for her. Men who had previously engaged her services would invariably return for more, a craving of which they had no desire to get rid; those deprived of that opportunity would seek her out on account of strong recommendations from her existing clients. It also did not hurt that she was skilled at sex. For that, she had her late husband to thank. He was constantly seeking new adventures, angles, role-plays, positions in that faculty so much so that she had acquired a suite of pleasure-heightening tricks throughout their many years together. For instance, should her client decide to hold back the climax for as long as he could, she would rough it out and pretend to enjoy the ordeal of being intromitted beyond the threshold of an average receiver, smiling through her pain and begging for more even if she knew it would leave her physically scarred and limp-legged in the denouement. In her mind, the overarching need to provide for her two sons and mother-in-law would always precede her existential distress.

❧

Not wanting to join a brothel knowing that a large portion of money paid by clients would eventually be siphoned by the matriarch of that establishment with only a pittance going to the girls providing the service, Mona decided to break out on her own, to go for broke. Besides, it was also the advice dished out by the same friend who had planted the seeds of prostitution in her mind when she was jobless and without money. Each night she would park herself at Crawford Street, the infamous belt of tarmac behind a forsaken warehouse where ladies of her trade would congregate. Sometimes, a pimp may approach her for some special lucrative assignments like the one she had just accepted which required her to spread a little love on some docked vessel.

Arriving half an hour early, she was fired up, all prepared to deliver her best because from what she understood, a handsome sum of money was waiting to be reaped. If things were to go smoothly, she would be able to buy new pairs of shoes for her sons and replace her mother-in-law's bone-breaking pallet with a more comfortable bed. On this late July night, there was even a hint of something tolerably unsure that agreed with her. She felt good. Optimistic even.

Led by a grease-stained deckhand, a friend of the pimp, to a relatively spacious room officially known as the Common Bunk with only one window looking out into the sea, she waited patiently for her clients to arrive, reportedly six men who would participate in the orgy. As a way of steeling her nerves before sex, Mona studied every item in the room. There were three wooden chairs lined up in a row against the wall, a rickety pool table, a mirror panelled across the entire expanse of the wall at the opposite end, a huge bed with a couple of pillows all fitted in dirty blue, and a light bulb dangling from the ceiling in the centre of the room. The floor was carpeted from wall to wall with a few cigarette butts left lying around. *Hmm, so this is the place for all their arranged orgies*, she reckoned. Judging from the size of the room, it was plausible to conclude that partakers of any romp would have more than enough space to move around without brushing against one another's elbows.

A humidity had stolen over the space, so she opened the window to let in some fresh air. Within a few minutes, the first sailor arrived. The instant he saw Mona sitting on a chair in her dress of seersucker blue, something overtook him. He immediately latched the door for no apparent reason that she could fathom.

'Lady, it's just going to be you and me. Now don't you worry cos I'm going to pay the additional amount owed to you by the rest of my gang,' he said, eyeing her with a lascivious smile. There was something about the light in the room, its dimness and the deepening yellow above her, that made his voice close, intimate. She took a good look at his face and quietly heaved a sigh of relief. For the first time, she found her client rather attractive, not that it mattered, since the job to her was merely a means to an end and she had learnt at the very outset to embrace the longs and shorts of male anatomies that came with the territory. She had also learnt to ride out the vagaries of body and breath odours with a self-imposed dollop of tolerance. Still, it would not hurt to be with a looker for a change, as many of her clients were out of shape or cursed with an inalienable wreck of a face or both. In contrast, this sailor had slightly curly hair with sideburns, a pair of soft lips, cheekbones that carried an air of masculinity, and a taut body with a deep tan. *Maybe he's lousy in bed, who knows for sure? Looks can be deceiving,* she mused.

The truth, unbeknownst to Mona, was this sailor wanted her all to himself, a desire far more intense and spontaneous than anything he had ever felt in his life. Even though it would cost him close to a month's pay, he had no qualms forking out the additional sum of money amounting to what his other five compatriots would have paid Mona had they not been shut out and compelled to move to the lower deck for the same kind of merrymaking. Hence, what was intended to be an all-out orgy would soon whittle down to a nookie between the sailor and Mona, an arrangement that sat well with her, as she had never been comfortable entertaining several men at one go despite the lure of a more attractive compensation.

'Well, that's fine as long as you pay me the agreed sum and you pay me now,' Mona said, the tone of her voice polite yet firm. The sailor moved towards her, retrieved a wad of notes from his pants pocket and handed it to her, eager to get the ball rolling so much so you could almost feel his heart leaping out of his chest. He introduced himself as Sean; she said her name was Lisa, preferring to work incognito at all times. And then he kissed her. Hard. He kissed her again, only to be interrupted by her request, at once gentle and unyielding, to count the money given to her and make sure she had been paid correctly before proceeding any further. She had since made it a point to demand for her remuneration ahead of any action, foreplay included, after being duped by a client who had refused to pay her following their session claiming she was not worth it despite his achieving an exciting earth-shattering exultation with more authenticity than alliteration.

While Mona was tallying the notes, the sailor wasted no time to get naked. Once she had squirrelled away the money into her bag, he lifted her up and carried her in one fell swoop to the bed in the room, an overture she perceived as more risqué than romantic but nevertheless a surprising manifestation, as no client had ever regarded her as a bride waiting to be swept off her feet literally. Again, he wasted no time to undress her—unzipping her dress, removing her bra, and peeling off her panties as though planet Earth may stop spinning altogether if he paused to take a breather. True to expectation, he found her just as attractive if not more irresistible without her clothes on, completely taken in by her full and handsome figure, apparently unmarred by parturition, her firm yet not overly large breasts and her skin as smooth as porcelain.

From that point onwards, she summoned every trick in her bag to please him. In her mind, she felt it would only be fair to satisfy him to the extent of what was humanly possible given that he had already shelled out a sum of money, of his own will nonetheless, equitable to what six clients would pay in total for her services.

'Wow, oh wow, aren't you something, my lady?' exclaimed the sailor who somehow managed to muster a respite in the thick of coitus to admire Mona, gazing at her face, caressing her tresses, still finding it hard to believe that he had taken full possession of her without having to share this gift with anyone else, their naked bodies enmeshed in a show of fluidity, one sliding against the other.

'Oh, you're making me blush,' Mona uttered in her part seductive, part flirtatious voice, furthering her charm in his sphere of admiration. If only he had heard her speak outside the confines of the room that they were in, away from her job to her sons and mother-in-law, he would not have believed even for a minute that it was the same person. Her actual voice was mostly shrill and a little on the soft side. She kept that under wraps whenever she was on the clock, trading it for a touch of voluptuousness. Not only was her voice fake, her oohs and ahhs were mostly fabricated and in her life outside of what she did for a living, she was relatively dull and unadventurous, certainly a galaxy away from being flirtatious. Whenever she contemplated the paradox, she could not help but detest her job. She detested the body weight of a stranger on hers; she detested having to feign her persona to please her clients; she detested her husband for leaving her in a lurch; most of all, she detested herself for what she had become.

Essentially, her work would always remain a battle between her own fierce will to keep her family afloat and the imprisonment of her true self, between the fire in her belly and the coldness of a stranger's touch, between her maternal sacrifice and its Faustian element. She knew that if she were to succeed professionally which meant securing an ongoing stream of income, she would have to strike a balance between closeness and distance, wantonness and forgiveness, her clients' needs and her own challenges.

'Lisa, tonight you're all mine,' the sailor reiterated, kissing her first on the mouth, followed by the neck down to her navel. And then he re-entered her, so rich and singular, so engorged with a mighty intensity that had hitherto been unstoppable, only to be waylaid by a pounding on the door accompanied by a gravelly shout: 'Open up, it's the police!'

❖

Jim Vincent heard some noise, peremptory, disapproving, unmistakably both male and female, as he leaned against the door. He tried opening it, but it was locked, obviously. Strains of 'Oh my god, this shouldn't be happening . . . don't worry, just jump out of the window into the sea . . . no, no, better jump now before it's too late' drifted within his earshot. Earlier, he had learnt from his second-in-command, Mohammed Noor, as well as one of the sailors caught flagrante delicto that another crew member might be in the Common Bunk together with a specially hired prostitute so he decided to check it out himself, reckoning he should be able to handle a pair of butt-naked culprits without neither much complication nor assistance. But it was not as straightforward as he had envisaged. The door happened to be a metallic one so he could not just ram it down with his body weight. At best, he could only pound on it as hard as possible, verbally threatening to break it open with gunshots if the people on the other side of the door were to continue to lock him out.

Inside the room, Mona and Sean the sailor rushed to clothe themselves and argued over whether to escape through the window, which meant jumping into the sea. She was bent on doing so, as she could not afford to get caught and be thrown into jail, not in a million years, and leave her children and mum-in-law to fend for themselves, and he refused to budge insisting there was no way on earth he could escape no matter what, since all crew members would have to be accounted for in times of a crisis or an unforeseen happening. Besides, he would probably get away with a mere stern warning from the authorities and continue to sail around the world unlike Mona who would end up incarcerated given that prostitution was illegal.

In the panic of the moment, Mona did not take into consideration the size of the window facing the sea, a circular aperture big enough at best to allow a mid-size dog to squeeze through. Nevertheless, she forced her way head first through it but was unfortunately held back by the girth of her hips, half her body dangling in the open, the other half getting stuck on the inside. Sean chuckled at her plight despite the general tension in the air. He did not mean to but it was too droll a scene to not be tickled by it. There she was, a reluctant victim of cruel, comic proportion.

'Pull me in!' she pleaded in desperation. He grabbed her hips and yanked her back into the room.

'I simply can't go to jail! Please help me, I'm begging you,' Mona said, hands pressing against her temples and half shielding her face from the shame of it all. 'Maybe you can tell them I'm your sister or a relative who's visiting.'

'At this hour? Not to mention testimonies from my fellow mates!' he shot back. 'I don't think they'll buy it.'

'Please . . . I promise to pay you back many folds in kind if you can just get me out of this,' she said with a despairing glint in her rheumy eyes. Meanwhile, the pounding continued, and it would only be a matter of time before the police knocked down the door with bullets and came barging in.

'Listen, this is what I'm going to do,' he said, holding her shoulders firmly with both hands. 'I'll open the door and I'll try to run away and the officer will do his best to stop me from escaping—I think he's the only person outside judging from the lack of commotion. Now, while he's struggling to keep me in his grasp, you need to run past us and away from this ship as fast as you can. Can you do that?'

She nodded, half thinking what a brilliant idea he had come up with, half recalling the last time she had actually sprinted which was decades ago when she was a child playing catch with her neighbours. She wondered how fast she could run at the present time, wishing she had done some sort of exercise in her leisure—maybe going for longer walks or gardening actively instead of sitting around and trying out one piece of jewellery after another—when her husband was still alive. Oh, how she missed those necklaces, bracelets, and rings she had to pawn in exchange for money to tide her family over! But she reminded herself now was not the best time for her to be addicted to easy luxuries of a halcyon past nor regret not keeping herself as fit as she would like to be. She had to prepare to run for her life.

'We'd better get moving before more policemen come knocking,' Sean said, holding her hand and pulling her towards the door. 'I'll count to three, open the door and you'll start running once I pretend to put up a fight with him, okay?' Mona nodded.

At the count of three, he did exactly just that. Jim Vincent, a strapping figure of Eurasian descent with biceps and pectorals hard enough to bounce off wayward houseflies, seized Sean by the neck as the latter struggled to break free. Mona held Jim's gaze steady for a moment, a crackle of social static between them. She had seen him many times in Lorong Limau, on a few occasions accompanied by his father Jude Vincent, the village chief. He did recognize her as well: the woman whose line of work had kept her from enjoying the same familiarity and warm intimacy that existed between the people belonging to the village, the woman whose presence halted conversations and prompted all kinds of expressions from sheepish to hostile, the mainstay of gossip among flibbertigibbets who had been haemorrhaging loose talk about how she had sold her soul to the devil and brought about the death of her husband. Further igniting poisonous glances in Mona's direction was Gau Pee who had taken liberty to spin a tale that had since spread like jubilant armies of fireflies casting a near-mystical shimmer on the village almost every night—she had told others Mona was having sex with underage boys and had warned parents to keep their teenage sons away from this 'seemingly docile but truly pernicious prostitute', usually speaking through the side of her mouth to other gossipers as she smiled her bitchy social smile whenever Mona happened to be within a few feet from her and a bunch of rumour-mongers. Of course, unbeknownst to Gau Pee at that point in time, she would later have to eat her words when she fell heedlessly in love with one of Mona's sons. But unlike some of his scatter-brained villagers, Jim Vincent knew better. He had heard the whole sad truth regarding Mona from his father.

Under normal circumstances, if a guilty party were to escape, Jim would have blown his police whistle to alert the rest of his flock so that they would come running and thwart the escape, but he merely watched Mona scamper off, not a sound of protest uttered, not a look of anger lodged. Granted he was keeping Sean in throttlehold before handcuffing him but there was something undeniably authentic about the way he had let her run away, his countenance betraying the subject of his thoughts. His outright sympathy for her had draped over him like a straitjacket as if to move an inch might invite the wrath of his inner voice, a separatist whose moral authority far outweighed its compassion for a hapless fellow villager. But how could he ever face himself in the mirror again if he were to order his men to arrest her, a poor woman who had sacrificed everything, her reputation, self-worth, and safety, to raise her sons and look after her visually impaired mother-in-law? He felt at peace letting her escape.

Even Sean was surprised that Jim showed no sign of anger or disappointment, a trait that would normally mark the faces of police officers in times like these. When subsequently asked by his second-in-command of the whereabouts of the call girl, Jim put paid to the case by saying that he had no choice but to let her escape, as he was too preoccupied wrestling with Sean at that time, calibrating his expression precisely between grave sense of duty and regret.

'We can try to come up with a drawing of her based on your memory,' said Mohammed Noor, the second-in-command.

Jim cleared his throat after his unmistakable little cough and then uttered in his lapidary fashion, 'I can't remember what she looks like. Everything happened so fast.'

Chapter Eight

Tin's family was in a shambles after Ah Hock's sudden, unexpected death. Her father was hardly in the house when he was supposed to be, at times returning home only in the wee hours of the morning, usually drunk and in a foul mood. Even his usual spouting of gan-ni-na had largely been absent from his vernacular, replaced by words pulled out of his throat in gruff, reluctant grunts. Gone were also his random pep talks on the correlation between money and filial piety. Deep down inside, he would have gladly swapped out Bok Koon for Ah Hock had he been given a choice to play God. One was his favourite, a striking resemblance to him in terms of physicality and temperament, the other nothing more than a source of embarrassment for being soft-spoken and introverted. In the end, he just could not summon the strength to survive the tragedy, succumbing to liver failure two years later caused by frequent bouts of alcohol consumption to which he resorted with the intent to numb his sorrow.

No one exemplified grief better than Tin's mother, a connoisseur of melancholy, having lost her newborns over the years to either adoption or death. Her shoulders slumped as she walked in public, her face a contorted expression of lugubriousness. Understandably so, since Ah Hock was her favourite after Gau Pee. She would always announce to everyone before a festive or celebratory meal where meat was going to be served that only Tin's father and Ah Hock could have the chicken thighs (poor Bok Koon was never in consideration despite being a guy in the family); she would give Ah Hock and Gau Pee the biggest *ang pows* (red packets containing money) every Chinese New Year; once she even readily forgave both of them—if it were Tin, she would have been cleaved alive—after learning that they had taken 'fake pictures' on the occasion of a relative's wedding; she would give him money each time he came up with the same sad excuse that he had overspent his salary; she would often tell relatives and neighbours none of her children mattered more than Gau Pee and Ah Hock, her 'gems from heaven'.

Bok Koon remained inscrutable in the wake of their family tragedy. As usual, he said nothing much; nor did he walk around the house in a state of Weltschmerz. Tin's father had many a times passed remarks alluding to his son's taciturn indulgence, echoing his displeasure as well as disappointment of siring a descendant who was so unlike him in all ways: 'Gan-ni-na, he would be the last person to dodge a falling sky', 'Gan-ni-na, can someone confirm if he does have balls?', 'Gan-ni-na, I sometimes want to just grab hold of his throat and rid it of the fish bone or marble or whatever that's stuck inside.' Anyhow, Bok Koon was never close to Ah Hock, not even by a blood-is-thicker-than-water stretch so no one would exactly call him out if he were to admit how little he was missing his brother.

Pao, who'd since moved out of the house after getting married, had always considered Ah Hock the male equivalent of Gau Pee—scheming, unrepentant, though not as malicious—so all she could summon for his untimely departure was to cry just a little at his funeral. Besides, she did not have much time to be saddled with grief what with a baby to take care of.

At least Bok Koon and Pao remained true to themselves in terms of expressing grief. Kee Kee, on the other hand, was nonplussed for the most part, not because she did not have it in her to feel sad but rather she was traumatized by the loss of income to her family—having been clueless about Ah Hock contributing peanuts—which she feared could potentially augur a tide of change: her family would now expect her to work in some way, be it helping out in the kitchen, sewing or knitting, responsibilities she had so far managed to abrogate. That fear would however last for only a couple of days, as she realized soon enough that everyone else in the family was simply not in the mood to pick a bone with one another, not to mention bark orders at her except in one instance when Tin's father almost had gan-ni-na at the tip of his tongue seeing his youngest daughter skipping and swaying in the house trying to imagine herself as a princess adored by the ogling masses.

The passing of Ah Hock was indeed a massive blow to Gau Pee. She cried for days on end and walked around like a tormented spectre on the verge of being relegated to the lowest depths of Hades. The weight of the tragedy had even transformed her witchy appearance into something more insufferable: swollen eye-bags (cried too much), collapsed cheekbones (ate too little), perpetual moue (either too much sadness or too little cursing). Moping about the house, she seemed to inhabit the air of a castaway who simply refused to be rescued.

For Tin, it was all about mourning the death of a brother despite many instances where he had ganged up with Gau Pee, no thanks to the latter's poisonous indoctrination, to upend her day-to-day existence, from spreading lies about her to magnifying her flaws and mistakes to a level of radioactive intensity. Case in point was when Tin had secretly taught a girl living in the same village how to sew and make a pair of samfu against her mother's self-serving instruction: 'It would be better for us marketability-wise if fewer people were to learn sewing.' Somehow Ah Hock had managed to catch wind of Tin's endeavour, making sure Gau Pee knew about it in order to pass this time-bomb-of-an-update to their mother. Naturally, their mother punished Tin by whipping her with a long cane until her skin was mottled with streaks of red. But what they chose not to share with Tin's mother was the fact that Tin was simply repaying the girl who had carried out an honourable deed by saving Kee Kee from falling into a pit which might have resulted in yet another death in the family. Instead of mitigating the severity of Tin's punishment, they merely smirked at the sight of their sister getting whipped, obviously enjoying the spectacle.

For all the pain Ah Hock had caused her, Tin was still crippled by the loss of her brother. His early death would forever steep her memory of him in pathos and nostalgia. Every night for hours, she waited for sleep. Her appetite was lacking, her mood sombre. She tried to focus on the positive aspects of their relationship, preferring not to dwell on the awful things Ah Hock had committed at her expense.

She remembered how often they had played together when they were kids, the gleefulness of that period in their lives unaffected by either family politics or Gau Pee's sleight of influence.

When she was cooped up in the home doing chores, she thought of him: the kind of food he enjoyed eating, the games he liked to play, his mannerisms, the way he dilated his eyes on purpose whenever a beautiful woman happened to walk past him. The more she thought of him, the more depressed she became. Only in the bright, open space of say, the market or the bus terminal, watching the world come together in a lattice of warm moving bodies, did she feel her old self stirring. The pick-yourself-up-after-a-fall Tin, the resolute Tin, the Tin who could see parts of the world click into shape like pieces in a jigsaw puzzle after a mishap or tragedy. For this reason, she did make it a point to get out of the house more frequently. For a while, nothing could possibly lift the heaviness in her heart. But what she did not know at that time was that there would be someone, a boy she fancied, entering her life thereafter, not only mowing down her heavy-heartedness but setting the stage for more upheavals in her family. Likewise, neither her bosom buddy Molly nor her dreadful sister Gau Pee could have predicted a common love interest at the forefront of their daily peregrinations . . . tantric, swooning. Then again, love was never meant to be straightforward for girls their age.

Despite the ongoing demurrals playing out in his head, Jim Vincent willed himself to draw a conclusion attributing Ah Hock's death to the recent flood. He had conducted several rounds of investigation at the Glorious Hole Brothel, after catching wind from friends of Ah Hock that he had, in fact, been a regular patron there, which eventually failed to produce any evidence of foul play, including homicide. Jim Vincent did make it a point not to disclose this piece of information to the family of the deceased; he just did not feel it was appropriate to let them know. As a matter of fact, it would have already been difficult for Tin's family to accept the sudden fate of Ah Hock let alone be further jangled with a knife-twist of his sullied nature far removed from their knowledge.

In the course of interrogating the matron of Glorious Hole, Jim did, however, suspect that something might be amiss, unable to connect the dots into a logical narrative even though in the end he really could not unearth any conclusive wrongdoing on her part.

'Oh yes, he was indeed a guest here the morning of the big flood,' the matron answered to Jim's query, her voice unwavering. 'But strangely he was adamant about leaving our premise for whatever reason soon after he was, uh, done resting in his room.'

'Resting in his room?' Jim queried in disbelief.

'Oh yes, resting in his room,' the matron answered without a hint of irony.

Jim listened to her every word, his eyes assessing every muscle fibre on her blemish-free face.

'Which of your girls were with him during his time here?' he asked. 'I need to talk to all of them.'

'Listen Mr Vincent, I'm running a respectable hotel and we don't—'

'Let's not kid ourselves, all right? You and I know what this place is all about despite what's stated in your sign so why don't you come clean with me for once? I'm not going to press charges on the illegality of your business, I'm here to find out exactly what happened to a man found dead in some pothole,' he said curtly.

'And I'm telling you I have no idea what you're talking about,' replied the matron sternly, refusing to budge.

'All right then, let me rephrase my question. Which lady or ladies did he happen to interact with from the time he checked in till the time he left?'

'As far as I know, he interacted only with me before he went to his room,' she said with a wry smile.

'Can I take a look at his room?'

'I'm sorry you can't. It's currently occupied. Do come back another time perhaps.'

'Did he say why he was leaving this place in the midst of a raging storm?'

'I don't know,' she answered with renewed nonchalance.

'You must also find it strange that his body had been retrieved somewhere very far from your brothel, I mean hotel,' he said, clearing his throat at the close of his sentence. 'I mean how could it be possible unless someone culpable must have engineered this and drove him ten miles to a place where he could almost never be found?'

'The flood must have something to do with it, I'm sure.'

'I wish I was as certain as you are, but based on past experience, no person, dead or alive, had been swept away by the waters to such a melodramatic extent, at least not here in Singapore.'

'Is there anything else I can help you with? I've got some business to take care of,' she asserted.

'No, that's all for now. Something tells me we'll probably see each other again.' Jim coughed, cleared his throat, and left Glorious Hole knowing the investigation had only just begun. In order to adhere to the investigation deadline after a couple of ensuing queries at the brothel, he proceeded to officially close the case and classify it as an 'accidental death'. But in all secrecy, he vowed to press on without telling his superiors and subordinates.

Meanwhile, Jim's string of visits had not rattled the matron much at all. She had expected all these and more and had repeatedly given clear instructions to her driver and the three women involved on what to say and how to act in front of enquiring police officers since the day they dumped Ah Hock's body near the sewers. Besides, she shielded them from any questioning as long as she could with the status quo intact until the day Jim Vincent decided to try a different tack altogether.

It was a relatively cool day, the tail end of the rainy season. The steady downpour earlier had given way to a trifling drizzle, persistent and frigid. The hawkers were out on the streets in Lorong Limau, red bean soup seller in one corner, *tahu goreng* in another, each one fanning the charcoal to start a healthy fire; children gathered around these makeshift stalls for their afternoon treats, faces mantled in anticipation, mood steeped in carefree laughter, undeterred by the slight drizzle. The noodle soup vendor was the first to open shop so naturally he got a head start. By the time the others managed to get their act together, he had already sold more than ten bowls, the few wooden stools surrounding his stall all fully occupied by patrons, each holding a bowl in one hand and chopsticks in the other, happily slurping down their noodles.

On the other side of the village with the river running through it, Tin and Molly and a host of others could be seen carrying pails and punnets and filling them up with *bua kee*s, a local breed of small black crabs that would spill over from the river to the levees following a heavy downpour and an ensuing high tide. Armies of bua kees would pulsate like undulating goosebumps on the riverbanks, the whole scene flickering in a near-mystical invasion of earth.

Meanwhile, Tin and Molly were too preoccupied scooping these bua kees into their respective pails to even take notice of Gau Pee striking up a conversation with a relatively good-looking guy, tall, strong, roughly the same age as her. As it turned out, he was Mona's oldest son, Chew Yong, who also happened to be catching bua kees with his younger brother Ming Hao. Obviously, he was trying to be polite, not wanting to immediately brush Gau Pee off after the latter had initiated the dialogue by introducing herself. For sure, he was not attracted to one who looked like a witch from some scary fairy tale. She, on the other hand, was working her charm on him, smiling coyly and stroking her forehand just to prove a point that she had flawless skin, and would have sooner died than admitted to anyone, herself included, that he was not even remotely interested in her what with his apathetic body language writ large.

'I have not seen you around here before,' Gau Pee commented in the form of a question after their mutual introduction by name. She squatted in front of him,

watching him gather the crabs that were scattering and
crawling in all directions.

'We moved here not too long ago,' he said, half looking
at her, half focusing his attention on the bua kees and filling
up his pail.

'We?'

'Yeah, I mean my family. That's my brother over there,'
he said, pointing to a guy also down on his knees a few feet
away, average built albeit slightly on the chubby side, pale
complexion, protruding ears.

'So, Chew Yong, what do you do for a living?' Gau Pee
asked, dwelling on her object of fancy and certainly not on
his younger brother who struck her as more introverted
than friendly, nary a smile from his face nor a display of
excitement from catching bua kees unlike the many boys
and girls around him shrieking, laughing and gesticulating to
the tune of fun. Moreover, she wanted to find out about his
'worth' on the assumption that most guys his age would have
probably been out of school and holding a job. Anything
above the status of clerks, primarily most jobs in an office or
a respectable institution, would sit well with her in terms of
husband material.

'I'll be graduating from university in a month's time,' he
replied with confidence, 'so until then I won't know the kind
of work I'll be doing.'

'Oh wow, this is great! A university grad!' she exclaimed
as if she were about to marry one. 'How I wish I'll be as smart
as you are in my next life.' He appeared nonplussed, gesturing
instead to his brother Ming Hao to buck up by showing him,
in a faux-mock manner, that his own pail had since been
filled to the brim with bua kees. With hardly any reaction

on his part, the younger one simply disregarded his older brother's teasing and continued gleaning the crustaceans at his own pace.

Disappointed that Chew Yong had not bothered to follow up on her remark with perspectives like 'I don't understand why girls are not given the chance to attend school' and 'It's a pity you have to wait till your next life to be able to study' which she was sure until a moment ago that he would, Gau Pee decided to rework her strategy to kindle his interest in her or at least in what she had to say.

'Your parents must be so proud of you. Imagine raising a son to become a university graduate!' she enthused with the sheer delight of someone winning the lottery. Of course, she did not know at this point in time that the very woman she had been badmouthing, branding her a slut and a whore, would turn out to be Chew Yong's mum.

'Thanks. What did you say your name was again?' He chose his words carefully with the intent of getting her off his back.

How dare he forget my name so quickly!

Gau Pee stopped short at showing her displeasure but instead manoeuvred herself into playing submissive, no doubt out of character, whispering her name in the most pretentiously coy manner with a little giggle at the end to sweeten her feminine appeal. He remained nonchalant, interrupting his accumulation of bua kees with a hollow, humdrum 'oh'.

Just then, something caught his eye, the image of another teenage girl who happened to be day to Gau Pee's night on the attraction scale. About ten feet away, she was also gathering bua kees rather frantically. He felt a stirring in his gut as he observed her tucking a strand of wayward black hair behind her ear. To no small degree did this sensation ripple through the other parts of his body till he could not help but smile the broadest of smiles while gazing in her direction. This girl seemed to be in a cheerful mood, laughing along with another girl by her side, probably her friend or sister.

As coincidence would have it, the girl to whom Chew Yong was attracted caught sight of his unspoken coquetry. She smiled back at him.

While all these were evolving, Gau Pee became an unwilling spectator by default. Barely able to conceal her feelings any more, her facial expression was suddenly exposed for what it was: a taut mask of pain and anger all rolled into one. She got the sinking feeling that she would never stand a chance with Chew Yong with this girl in the picture, someone whom she happened to loathe to bits. From that point onwards, she swore to make whatever romance might develop between these two persons a helluva hellhole.

It turned out to be a productive day for both Tin and Molly. They had a smashing time by the river, filled their respective containers to the brim with bua kees and, much to their delight, made friends with boys who could potentially initiate a romantic trajectory with them. On their way home, they talked about their new friends. Molly confessed about being smitten with Chew Yong, having taken notice of him at a distance prior to their initial exchange of words though not fully realizing he had felt the same way about her; she was also thrilled he had approached her to introduce himself, not realizing he had secretly seized the opportunity to take leave of a rather disgruntled Gau Pee who had cleaved to him as though he were already her steady boyfriend. In the same instance, Tin was introduced to Ming Hao by Chew Yong who had publicly bestowed the title of 'the thinker in our family' on his younger brother. He had struck her as being less self-possessed compared to Chew Yong and definitely more huggable owing to his slight pudginess. Strange but true, Tin had always been drawn to the latter aspect in men, a trait that was glaringly absent in her family tree, as everyone from Tin's parents, uncles and aunties to her siblings and cousins turned out to be skinny or at best lean. Perhaps it was safe to assume that one might be attracted to qualities and characteristics lacking in one's surrounding. In her case, chubbiness equated bear-hugs. Indeed, she could always use a hug from time to time, especially after receiving a dressing-down from Gau Pee or her father. All in all, she thought well of Ming Hao based on first impression.

Once they got home, Tin and Molly no longer had the luxury to dwell on their newfound friends. Tin was expected to prepare the bua kees for consumption; Molly had to first help her mother weave baskets to be sold and then attend to the marination of bua kees. Arguably, hauling that windfall of crabs back home might just have been the best part of their day. Not only was it free of charge but it also helped break the monotony of eating porridge and pickles day-in, day-out.

Since Gau Pee was not at home, Tin decided to marinate the bua kees on her own, first depositing them—still very much alive—in a large wooden bin, then pouring soya sauce over them and stirring the mix with a spatula. She would then slice a couple of red chillies, toss them into the bin and continue with the stirring. About twenty minutes into the marination, she would cover the bin with a tight lid and let the bua kees die a slow death supposedly over a two-day period. After that, they would be ready for consumption albeit uncooked technically in the most ironic sense. Initially, Tin was at odds with the process of 'cooking' these crabs first taught to her by her late grandmother. She found it cruel, even nauseous at one point. But over time she had gotten used to it, propelled inevitably by her family's financial situation.

Most Singaporeans would swear by the bua kees' simultaneously acquired and mainstream taste, peeling off the shells and wolfing down the flesh, yam-like in terms of texture and palatability. There might be a handful who would fall prey to diarrhoea after eating them, unable to stomach the rawness of the dish but for the majority, it would be nothing short of gastronomic de rigueur.

By the time Tin was done marinating the crabs as well as cooking dinner for the day, it was already close to evening. The villagers had mostly exhausted the questioning and answering of the one thing that was practically on everyone's lips: 'Did you catch a lot of bua kees?' The sun was lingering on the horizon, birds were flying northwards, workers were leaving their workplaces and returning home for dinner, the day was beginning to plateau into a shimmering stillness, poised for its descent into darkness. In that quiet interlude between day and night, Ming Hao entered Tin's consciousness in all of his wordless, understated virtuosity.

There were no more floods. The rainy season was on the wane. This morning, the rain had given way to scudding cirrocumuli, leaving in their wake bursts of bright sunshine melding with blustery wind. Clumps of fallen leaves had remained stuck in patches of mud, patinae of water had mantled fields within and outside Lorong Limau.

Sobered by the cool air, Mona woke up earlier than usual. The house felt empty. Her two sons had since left for school; Chew Yong, the older one, was studying in Nanyang University; Ming Hao, two years younger than his brother, was about to take his O Levels soon. The only one around was Mona's mother-in-law who would stay in bed most of the time, hamstrung by her blindness and hence the lack of mobility in the house. The times she needed to be somewhere, at the dinner table, in the toilet, or just sitting on a rocking chair outside their shack, she would be assisted as well as accompanied by either Mona or one of her grandsons and if both parties were not present, she would mostly lie in bed and wait for either to get home.

After the debacle on the ship a few nights ago, Mona just wanted to do something uplifting today to nullify the trauma she had experienced on that fateful occasion, remembering how close she was to being arrested and locked up had it not been for Jim Vincent's misstep. Was it a genuine misstep or something else altogether? Did he happen to go lax on her just because she was a fellow villager? She could not tell for certain although she did have an inkling of Jim's compassion judging from his demeanour. She had often seen him help the elderly cross the street and carry heavy items on behalf of the pregnant and the infirmed. Still, the possibility of facing arrest continued to tug at her mind, since Jim Vincent knew very well where to find her given that they lived a few blocks away from each other.

The thought was starting to depress her, so she quickly switched mental gears. No doubt she needed an uplift. Towards that end, she decided to shop for gifts for everyone in her family using part of the money she had pocketed that night, the sole bright spot amid the charred deck of memories. It would be like an approximation of her old life, her old joie de vivre, her old spirit of giving when her husband had been alive, when she could comfortably exact material pursuit.

She was deliberating between a long-sleeve, white cotton shirt and a pair of leather shoes for Chew Yong, whose university graduation was just around the corner, and had her mind fixed on comics for Ming Hao and a butter cake with chocolate frosting for her mother-in-law. It was about time she surprised them beyond meal provisions. If questioned, she would justify her action by lying about receiving a financial bonus from her boss ('I work as a clerk in a small office,' she had told her mother-in-law and sons.) Sometimes, she wondered if her sons had already caught wind of her real profession from all that village gossip about her which had been tossed around. That she had to go back to the office on most nights to 'clear the backlog', an excuse that had been regurgitated to the point that it just could not be taken seriously at face value any longer except maybe by naive children, would certainly not be considered above suspicion by any stretch. But for now, she would put that thought aside, dress up in one of her favourite outfits, a white chiffon dress with petal motifs, inform her mother-in-law that she was heading out of the house and make her way to Chinatown by bus. Feeling the way she had been, it appeared as if she was about to embrace a perfect day. Sadly, it was anything but.

The moment she landed in Chinatown after a rickety bus ride, she ran into Jim Vincent of all people who also happened to be shopping in the same area. At first, she did not know what to do, whether to avoid him for fear of being apprehended or just walk past him mouthing a quiet 'thank you'. Either way, it got her all tensed up. Before she could decide on her course of action, Jim Vincent had already started walking towards her, brisk and focused.

He was not wearing his police uniform, so she was inclined to believe that he was off-duty and had no formal authority to arrest her. If need be, she would even deny her presence on the ship that night, since only a few people—Jim Vincent, Sean the sailor, and the deckhand who had ushered her into the room—knew about her visit and from what she had heard, Sean had been let off the hook and the ship had since sailed off, which meant no one else could testify against her. It suddenly dawned on her that it would be Jim Vincent's word against hers and with that, she felt slightly more settled. She decided their chance encounter be stripped of any requirement for courtesy, much less any room for a cursory nod of acknowledgement.

'I was planning to look for you in the village,' Jim Vincent said upon confronting her and without warning, grabbed her by the arm and led her to one of the quieter, people-less back alleys in Chinatown. She trembled, her body instantaneously drained of vigour, face leached of colour.

'Ouch, you're hurting me,' she moaned once he came to a halt.

Jim Vincent released his grip on her arm and backed off a few steps.

'I'm sorry,' he said, more indifferent than remorseful.

'Do I know you?' she questioned, pretending she had never seen Jim Vincent for the life of her.

He stared at her, a glowering look in his eyes, jaw muscles twitching, and said, 'I usually tell people I don't arrest anyone that doesn't deserve it but I'm willing to adjust my philosophy if they're willing to help me test it.'

Mona froze momentarily, her sheath of pretence slipping off. Jim Vincent continued staring at her, gimlet-eyed. There was this silence that fell like a dead weight between them. Like a piece of china about to drop on to the floor, she could barely contain her fragility. Her breath came short and shallow, her eyes moist with tears, her palms began to sweat. Earlier in the day, she had thought her brush with the law on the ship and her subsequent escape might just end up as a final chapter unto itself but now it was beginning to assume the form of a penultimate narrative. In all probability, Jim Vincent appeared set to imprison her. Her only chance now, slim as it might seem, was to run away from him as fast as she could.

But instead of running away, she started wailing, crumbling onto the ground. A few people sauntered into the otherwise empty alley to check out what was happening after hearing her piercing cry. Jim Vincent firmly deflected their curiosity with his palm.

'Please give us some privacy. My wife is having a mental breakdown and I need to handle this,' he shouted across the alley to the few bystanders. Soon, they walked away, not wanting to be involved in the intrigues of strangers.

'I can't go to prison, I simply can't,' she spoke in the midst of all that lamentation.

'You're not going to prison,' he told her, placing his hands on her shoulders as a gesture of affirmation. Hearing that, she immediately stopped crying and shot him a perplexed look. 'But I need you to do something for me.'

'I'm not going to prison?' She stood up.

He shook his head.

'Oh,' she uttered, equal parts surprised and sentient. 'In that case, I'm sure we can work something out.' Her smile suggested she had an inkling of the type of favour Jim Vincent was referring to. At first, she had her doubts, perceiving Jim Vincent as a police chief who was supposedly above bribery, but those doubts evaporated soon as she likened him to most other men with a robust appetite for sex. Spurred by her own thesis, she started tracing the tightness of his chest with her fingers running down his shirt and whispering to him, 'I have no objection to a strong muscular man, still less to being invited to keep one happy.'

But she could not have been more wrong. Sex was not even part of the equation. That he had let Mona escape from the ship, his compassion trumping rectitude at that point in time, had only bruised him with guilt. Even though he knew he had done something empathetic, some would even say commendable, for a pitiful fellow villager and that he would not have hesitated to act any differently given a repeat scenario, he found it especially hard to forgive himself for the professional lapse committed on purpose.

'You're clearly mistaken,' he said, pushing her hand away from his body. He took the next few minutes explaining to her what was on his mind. She listened, hanging on to every word he was saying.

He added, 'If you live up to your end of the bargain, I will forget we even met on that ship.'

In Lorong Limau, almost everyone knew one another by name and was familiar with all the great-grandmothers' tales so it did not take long for Gau Pee to find out about Chew Yong's family. The most unsettling part of her revelation, of course, rested on the identity of his mum. She just could not believe the woman whom she had been aspersing all this while had turned out to be the mother of a cheerful, handsome guy whom she fancied but who seemed to have been wrenched from her grasp by her arch-rival Molly—a glaring manifestation of her ego-fuelled persona which made her believe Chew Yong had been tricked into loving another woman rather than admit he just was not into her.

One thing was for sure, she vowed to take back what she considered to be hers. It was obvious Molly was not going to be her only obstacle. She reckoned Mona, Chew Yong's mother, would be a linchpin in her game plan so naturally she would do all that was humanly possible to reverse her standing in Mona's books and gradually win over her consent. But first, she must find a way to neutralize or better yet over-compensate for the many nasty things she had said about her in public—the sluttiness, the shameless whoring.

That opportunity presented itself one desultory afternoon when Gau Pee ran into Mona by chance at the entrance to the British barracks while delivering a stack of name tags she had sewn for the army personnel. Mona, in a tight red dress, presumably after her work appointment with some officer, since officers had more leeway to engage call girls during office hours, was about to leave the premise just when Gau Pee was about to enter. Mona could not help but wince at the sight of the latter hanging vaguely in her consciousness as one of the gossipy villagers often seen lingering near the market and verbally jabbing at everyone from grandmothers to toddlers. Her spontaneous reaction to Gau Pee was owing more to a close-up of the sorceress incarnate—*oh my, that nose*—than to her being the initiator of tittle-tattle. She almost allowed her face to bunch up in grimace but thought better of it, simply looking down at the floor to avoid any further eye contact and hoping to lope away from her.

'You must be Mona, right? I've been wanting to get to know you for the longest time ever!' Gau Pee exclaimed, trying to disarm her with honey-dripping intent.

You can imagine the shock that reverberated down Mona's spine when she was confronted. At first, she thought Gau Pee was going to either cast a spell on her—*who knew if she truly had witchy powers, for she certainly looked the part*—or troll for more gossip-worthy titbits like what she had been doing in the barracks dressed in a tight-fitting luminous outfit with a wink and a smile to match the obviousness of her query. Luckily, it turned out to be neither witchcraft nor angling although it still was not clear to her at that point why she had suddenly been stopped in her tracks.

Gau Pee then took liberty to lift Mona's hand to shake it and introduced herself with the same faux coyness that had greeted Chew Yong when he met her for the first time by the river.

Looking at her face up close once again and hearing that plangent yet calibrated voice of hers, Mona was suddenly struck with an unequivocal jolt of the mind: Gau Pee was indeed the main perpetrator of all the hurtful blows directed at her—*how she ought to be ashamed of herself for conducting her meretricious activities*—whenever their paths intersected—Gau Pee invariably leading a group of rumour-hungry women and Mona dodging their bullets coated with open dishonour. She now recalled this very girl cursing at her on a specific occasion when she had been at the bakery, calling her 'big slut' repeatedly to the giggles of other villagers around them.

'Uh, what do you want from me?' Mona asked point-blank, disregarding any niceties to be had, what with her abrupt revelation.

'Oh, I just want to let you know how beautiful you are. You're probably the prettiest woman in Lorong Limau,' Gau Pee said, pretending to be starry-eyed.

Stumped for words, Mona cocked her head in bewilderment. She was still figuring out what to make of this girl. Having been wont to diatribes from gossipers like her—come to think of it, no one had been as scathing as she—it now seemed dangerously odd to witness the pendulum swinging to the other end. *Has Gau Pee brought her power of selective forgetfulness to bear on their chance meeting?* she wondered. To dispel the awkward vibe, she murmured a thank you.

Taking it as a cue that Mona might be more or less receptive to her accosting, Gau Pee launched into a cavalcade of apologies, saying how sorry she had been for misjudging her, for not empathizing with her financial circumstances, and most of all for vilifying her in public.

'I feel terrible, I mean should have never said all those things about you. I hope you'll find it in your heart to forgive me. Trust me, I'm not a bad person,' Gau Pee said meekly, weighing the reaction on Mona's face.

At that last sentence, Mona felt equal parts hilarity and disbelief, much like being told you can cavort around tigers in the wild and still get away alive if not unhurt. She smiled faintly, trying to mask the look of ridicule on her face, knowing for a fact that an apology had been made ex nihilo yet finding it hard to believe that vindictiveness could so readily morph into compassion.

'Tell you what,' Gau Pee continued, interpreting Mona's half-smile as a sign of her forgiveness, 'I'll drop by at your place someday to let you have a taste of my home-made butter tarts. You're going to love them.' She beamed like a girl about to married off to a tycoon.

'Sure, but you really don't have to,' Mona replied hesitantly. 'Look, I have to go.' On that note, she scarpered back to her house, walking as nimbly as she could, at the same time emptying her thoughts associated with the terrifying image of a malevolent witch as though any minute lost in doing so might cause it to persist in her mind with undiminished clarity.

Chapter Nine

Mona was being paid a monthly stipend by Jim Vincent for going under cover at the Glorious Hole Brothel (or Hotel as the owners and staff would insist). She was expected to work there a few hours each day as a freelance agent with the intent of cosying up to the matron and the rest of the women so as to wring out any insider information surrounding Ah Hock's death. In the course of her first week, she had managed to uncover the identity of the three key witnesses, the same women who stayed and frolicked with Ah Hock in the room before he was abandoned to rot away at some faraway gutters. Two of the women were rather tight-lipped; the last of the trio, the youngest and skinniest one, appeared to show more cracks, as she would lower her head in contrition and walk away quietly each time Mona happened to talk about the unfortunate incident. It went without saying that all three had been instructed by the matron not to breathe a word about it to anyone, police and otherwise.

One morning though, while Mona was tending to the room after her client had left, the skinny girl approached her unexpectedly to ask her how she had been adjusting to her new environment. Seeing that this might be the opportunity to troll for a few pertinent details, possibly incriminating evidence in line with Jim Vincent's suspicion, Mona wasted no time to pursue a lengthier conversation with her.

Adjourning to the brothel's kitchen, they sat down at a circular wooden table with a white marble top, drank some tea, and talked about their lives in general. Mona listened attentively as the skinny girl rambled on about how she had been trying to set herself up for marriage hopefully to a decent and relatively well-to-do guy so that she could afford to quit her line of work once and for all. Unfortunately, she had not been lucky enough to even take that first step, as every matchmaker, it seemed, had turned her down knowing somehow that she had been working in the Glorious Hole Hotel despite her every attempt to bury reality. She also told Mona that she had been an orphan all her life raised by a kind old spinster who had since passed on and like her listener sitting across the table from her, she was not skilled in everyday tasks such as cooking, laundry, and sewing, work associated with women in general, so she resorted to selling her body to earn her keeps. Her stories were often meandering and hard to follow, in the middle of which Mona had to press her fingers firmly against her temples to parry the onslaught of a massive headache. Of course, the skinny girl mistook Mona for being rapt in her stories.

Outside, the soft wind, surreptitious and whispery, drifted past the outreached Angsana trees. Nowhere to be seen was the usual gaggle of market-going women, either at home busy preparing rice dumplings for the upcoming Spring Festival or undertaking part-time jobs to earn extra money to make these dumplings. The majority of people on the streets were the breadwinners— the men—walking or cycling to work, the overwhelming sounds the squeak of their shoes, their bicycle bell rings and the rattle of buses plying the island's town centre.

At some point, the skinny girl began probing Mona about her private life, whether she was married, why she had become a prostitute, and how well she was coping with life in Lorong Limau. Soon enough, they bonded over an exchange of stories about the times they would cry in private after being ill-treated by their clients, something they knew nobody outside their trade would have been able to empathize. Amid the seemingly downcast dialogue, both women did have a few laughs though over what they perceived as comeuppance for their clients. The skinny girl recounted an incident where her customer had almost choked to death while performing cunnilingus, strands of her pubic hair tangled up inside his throat; Mona limned the story of how one of her clients had allowed his ice cream to melt, prematurely, the moment she held his cone in her hands, much to his annoyance not to mention full-on embarrassment.

Throughout this time, Mona was waiting for the right moment to broach the subject of Ah Hock. And she felt there was no better time than during their jocular moments to crack an opening before the skinny girl embarked on yet another round of her meandering personal stories.

'I'm not sure whether you will find this funny or cruel but once I was with a guy who happened to suffer a heart attack and collapse in my arms during sex,' said Mona, fabricating a tale which she hoped would evoke a response from the skinny girl, purposely drawing parallels with one of Jim Vincent's theories of what might have happened to Ah Hock which meant he could have died in the brothel prior to being found near the sewers.

'What? Are you serious?' asked the skinny girl, a flicker of feigned disbelief in her eyes.

'It's all true. At first, I thought he'd simply fallen asleep because maybe he found me boring or something. But when I couldn't wake up him by all means, I started getting worried and immediately called for an ambulance.'

'Oh wow,' the skinny girl muttered, obviously adrift in her own thoughts.

'It's tragic, isn't it?' Mona said. 'I'm not sure why but somehow I felt a bit guilty about the whole incident.'

The skinny girl nodded her head slowly in agreement. She seemed on the verge of saying something, but no words came out of her mouth.

'You look lost. Is everything okay?' Mona asked without betraying her real intent.

'Ugh, I . . . I mean . . . there's been a similar incident right here although I'm not supposed to talk about it . . . I don't know . . . I'm kind of confused, guilty,' she said, unsure if she should be continuing with what she had started.

'Oh gosh I'm so sorry. What happened? You seem rather affected by it,' said Mona, blatantly showing her concern.

'To be honest, the guy didn't die of a heart attack. In fact, he—'

'Well, well, well, here you are. I was looking high and low for you ladies.' The voice of the matron boomed into existence. Startled, both Mona and the skinny girl sprang up a little from their seats. Mona wondered if she had been lurking by the kitchen all this while eavesdropping on their conversation. However, the matron gave nothing away in her facial expression.

'There's an important gentleman waiting in the courtyard, and he would like to take a look at all our women before making his pick,' she said. Late forties, hair as wiry as creepers, fleshy earlobes, lips the distinct colour of Beaujolais, the matron was of a plump build beneath a green-and-yellow caftan. 'Finish your tea quickly and meet me in the courtyard.' Her voice had a biting edge on which you could possibly slice your thumb.

'And you!' said the matron, facing the skinny girl after Mona had left the kitchen. 'Wipe that stupid, guilty look off your face!'

Tin's family was still steeped in bereavement. After all, it had only been six weeks since the sudden passing of their oldest son Ah Hock; the house had become depressingly dour, as matter of fact as watching wallpaper peel off. No one could muster a smile—at least not in a natural way, with the exception of Kee Kee who would sometimes appear gleeful at the random thought of her marrying an aristocrat one day. No one admitted to sleeping well. No one spoke much. They kept schtum during meals and mostly retreated to their own cocoons once they were done eating. Guarded, constrained, timorous, everyone went around each other on tiptoes, murmuring, deferring, agreeing, more often than not letting silence take hold of their time together. Submerged in the murky depths of grief, they seemed to be withholding their fullest selves.

That they were officially expected to mourn for one hundred days, a Chinese custom inherited from generations past, made it impossible for them to not observe a code of conduct commensurate with respect for the deceased. For instance, donning outfits in colours other than black and white would be frowned upon as would seeking pleasure from watching outdoor operas and dancing to loud music. Anyone seen with his head thrown back in raucous laughter during a conversation or heard singing a song while taking a bath would surely be given no end of chastisement. Overt sadness happened to be the new mascot, quietude the new cheerleader.

Gau Pee, in a rare display of vulnerability, had been grieving for her closest sibling—Ah Hock was a true comrade whereas Kee Kee was just an ally she could manipulate—by suppressing her usual desire to condemn or gossip about other villagers. For a while, it seemed like nothing could possibly help her snap back to life except perhaps if Molly were to drown herself in the Singapore River.

But shortly after, she heard from the grapevine that Molly had been seeing Chew Yong rather often and the thought of her nemesis spending time with her fantasized paramour managed to not only blunt her grief but set into motion her febrile gust of determination to decimate their relationship. In a heartbeat, she very much reclaimed her old persona, this time fortifying her authority vis-à-vis her brother's passing. If any of her siblings were to so much as share a joke within earshot or shut the door a tad too loud, she would cast them a sinister gimlet look, embedded in which would be the message that they were showing little respect to Ah Hock and should instead be moping around, stony-faced, languid of character. Outsiders were not spared either. She would not hesitate to bark at anyone who laughed or appeared merry in her presence like the time when these twin sisters who lived two blocks away from her had been queuing up for water with Gau Pee at the faucet point and broke into giggles over a chat about some effeminate boys in the village. In a withering response, she splashed water at them from a pail that had been filled up by the first person in the queue and yelled, 'Don't you have any respect for the dead? My family is still grieving and here you are gossiping about the girlies. How audacious!' The twins hung their heads in embarrassment and exited the scene as quickly as they could while the rest of the crowd gave her the overwrought 'I'm so sorry for your loss' look which she had been receiving over the weeks and had obviously not outgrown the attention that came with it.

But the irony of it all was that she—more than anyone else—turned out to be most relieved at the conclusion of the hundred-day mourning period. You could suddenly sense the slackening in the air around her as though she had been waiting ever so desperately to liberate herself from all that doom and gloom.

The hot season had finally arrived. The soft blue–grey of overcast skies was now replaced by crimson–orange of sun flares. A feeling of tepidity and lethargy suffused the country. Here in Lorong Limau, young boys walked around topless, children took longer afternoon naps, women fanned themselves with heart-shaped rattan fans in group gatherings while roosting atop wooden fences demarcating one's backyard from another's. Something inert, familiar, absent was afoot.

The heat had become so unbearable that many felt compelled to leave their sun-strangled houses for a swim in the river or a loll under huge, shady trees in the field.

Some like Tin and Molly planned an outing to New World Entertainment at Jalan Besar, a carnival of sorts filled with music, games, and performances, merely to distract themselves from the heat.

When Kee Kee learnt about Tin's outing to New World, she insisted on not only joining her older sister but also tried to wangle a free entry for herself.

'You know I have no money. I don't sew clothes or make tarts like you do, so how am I supposed to come up with the entrance fee of fifty cents?' Kee Kee asked in a faux self-pity mode. 'The question is not whether you have the means to pay for me but rather if you want to or not.'

Kee Kee was spot-on in her argument. Tin did have some money put aside from whatever paltry allowances were given to her as a result of her contribution to the family income through the making of tarts and the sewing of clothes, an adjudication jointly set in motion and served by Tin's mother and Gau Pee.

'But if I were to pay for you, then I will have nothing left in my savings,' replied Tin, proving that nothing would throw their state of poverty into starker relief than the time it had taken her—more than six months—to amass just a dollar.

'Oh, please Tin! Please! Please! Please! I've never been to New World!' Kee Kee pleaded, knowing it would take less time for her sister to relent than for her to mentally plan her make-believe wedding to some prince.

'All right then but promise me you'll behave yourself when we get there,' said Tin, feeling oddly happy to be able to foot the bill for her sister, despite the depletion of her piggy bank.

'Ooh, thank you, thank you. Maybe I'll finally get discovered over there by some film producer who would groom me to become a star. What do you think?' Kee Kee quipped.

'I doubt you'll ever find a movie producer at New World.'

Tin was right. New World was never a playground for the rich and famous. It was more for the likes of Molly and Tin and also Chew Yong and Ming Hao (who had to be persuaded to join the gathering), a group of teenagers from working class families.

Two big lion statues made of cement guarded the gate to New World Entertainment, one on each side, short of a growl on their faces yet as predatory as one might envisage. Chew Yong and Ming Hao were already waiting at the gate when Tin, Molly, and Kee Kee arrived. Tin introduced the brothers to Kee Kee; the latter wasted not a minute more to add a pinch of glamour to her profile by emphasizing her mystical antecedence in all things royalty ('That's why it's probably a flaw in God's plan to make me the daughter of a proletarian.')

'Ooh there's the teacup ride over there! You know where to find me then,' Kee Kee said to the gang following her introduction, prancing away like a ballerina with faux grace.

'Don't forget to meet us here in an hour's time!' Tin cried out at her younger sibling, her tone a tentative mix of command and helplessness.

At this time, Chew Yong and Molly also took leave of the group to harvest their love nest, leaving Tin and Ming Hao to their own whims. Both Chew Yong and Molly decided to first try out the Ghost Adventure, a ten-minute ride on an open tram coursing through a softly lit grotto with apparitional figures popping up at intervals to frighten the hell out of patrons. Cliché as it might sound but Chew Yong and Molly were more game for a cuddle rather than the ride itself. Since it was frowned upon for couples, married and otherwise, to display intimacy in public other than holding hands, the best places thus to take intimacy to the next level was enclosed areas like cinemas and of course the infamous Ghost Adventure. The cuddling felt so right, so aligned with the universe that they decided to take the ride a few more times.

Throughout the evening, as they walked around New World, participating in various games such as spank the popped-up monkey and trying out other rides, they weaved in and out of conversational details about each other and their respective families. She shared with him, among other things, her desire to pick up driving skills one day (she did obtain her driving license in later years after marriage) even though she acknowledged she would most likely not be able to afford a car in her lifetime. Chew Yong listened attentively without interruption, nodding his head once every few sentences. She also told him how she would have given anything to travel overseas just for once.

'Listen, I'll be finishing my studies here in a few weeks' time and I'm currently awaiting news about my overseas scholarship for my master's programme. It's probably going to be in Germany,' said Chew Yong. 'I'm thinking perhaps you can take this opportunity to visit me. I mean I'll find a way to pay for your airfare so you won't have to worry about that.'

Molly of course had other concerns apart from the financial aspect of the proposal. How could she ever bring herself to leave her mother and siblings—even if it were for a short period of time—whose lives were more or less suspended in penury? And to possibly live in the same apartment with a man she knew for a mere couple of months, more so to whom she was not married? What would her mother say about this? She could only assume the worst, rightfully so.

Although they'd had sex a few times prior to this outing, neither party would seriously harbour the notion of marriage anytime soon. He had studies to pursue, and she mouths to feed. Their trajectories converging would be like squeezing the hands of fate. Moreover, both Chew Yong and Molly— unlike the society at large—had never regarded sex outside marriage as something to be frowned upon or as a taboo subject to be spoken of only in murmurs and gossipy aspersions or more importantly as an incontrovertible lead-in to conjugal vows. For him, he had clearly set himself apart from other men who still foundered in what he saw as the trappings of an outworn age and would only want to marry virgins. That his father had passed on without warning had, by his own admission, something to do with his easy-going disposition and his attitude towards most things in life including sex. 'Life is short, unpredictable, and happiness could be wrenched away at any moment for reasons out of our control,' Chew Yong would often say to Molly with a half-smile and a twinkle in his eye.

The first instance when he and Molly were about to get undressed in a deserted field just outside the precincts of Lorong Limau, he had questioned her a few times to make sure they were in sync and realized that his notion of sex chimed well with her own fancy of pleasure. By the time they lapped up each other on repeat mode, there was no stronger evidence of the absence of guilt or regret than that the subject of marriage never being broached by either party vis-à-vis what they had been savouring.

For Molly, she had not counted on her time spent with him going any further than a couple of intense but sporadic frolics on the grass and his eventual departure from Singapore. *He could have any girl he wants what with his education and looks and he's certainly too good for me*, she would often remind herself, setting up the stage where she would bid farewell to him with minimal heartbreak.

'I would love to go overseas with you, but you know I can't,' she said, half stuttering.

'Why? Is it money that's holding you back? Like I said, I'll find a solution.'

'No, it's not just about money.'

It was already 8 p.m. and the burgeoning crowd muscled its way into queues for the popular rides in New World. Many were also enjoying the live concert by a group of unheard-of singers. Chew Yong and Molly were sharing a bench with another couple outside the one and only vinyl shop in the premise and drinking from the same packet of sweet, coloured beverage that he had bought earlier after their Ghost Adventure rides. Coloured drinks were rather popular with the masses at that time, a concoction of water mixed with syrup stored in large, ice-cold glass containers. The added syrup could be red, green, or yellow depending on the source of colouring. Molly especially had taken a shine to the taste of the drink from the moment she first dipped her tongue into it at a cousin's wedding reception.

'What else is on your mind?' he asked, looking the part of someone about to solve the most complex riddle.

'I don't know . . . it's a host of other things I guess,' she said with a rueful smile, something less of unwillingness than of guilt, watching him weather her onslaught of improbability.

'You know what?' he held her hand accompanied by a cheeky grin on his face, his playfulness in full throttle.

'What?'

'Let's get married then.'

'You're kidding, right?'

'Says who?'

She remained stumped, unable to get a word out of her system like she had been strangled there and then.

'Besides, the travel expense of my wife will be fully covered by the scholarship council. But that's not why we should get married. I want to marry you because I just can't imagine otherwise.'

Tin and Molly made it a point to chat at their usual meeting place after their excursion to New World. Sitting on a straw mat—frayed around its edges—which they had been rolling out on the field outside their block for their regular evening get-together, they started sharing with each other about what had taken place earlier, combing the eidetic contours of their respective conversations with the brothers. The village's cosy otherness would always appear to be heightened in the late evening with several pockets of people like Tin and Molly chatting away in the same venue, a vast featureless landscape with nothing save acres of grass. As usual, the air was humid. Candle-lit rooms appeared through gaps in leafy trees, susurrations of the gentle breeze caressed the ears.

What was shared by Tin could not have been more different from the subsequent account by Molly, owing much to the contrasting personalities of the brothers themselves: one was sociable, playful, and prone to laughing, the other quiet, sombre, and not given to humour. Tin's time spent with Ming Hao had turned out to be rather excruciating. Prior to their meeting at New World, they had met only once by the river where they were catching bua kees alongside Molly, Chew Yong, and Gau Pee so she could not truly say she knew him well except that she was attracted to him in a peculiar, offbeat manner. His airtight quietude which Tin had initially found to be such a tonic in small doses had grown to be toxic, consuming their entire evening altogether at New World. She would ask him something, he would answer pithily. Whenever she made a random comment that was not about anything in particular such as the crowdedness or the bright colours of balloons everywhere, he would merely nod his head, expressionless, inscrutable. Not even halfway through their little outing, Tin had found herself cornered by her own gut feeling about speaking only out of necessity like 'Should we try this ride?' or 'I need to go to the restroom', if only to avoid making Ming Hao feel more uncomfortable than he already was—at least that was what she thought— and to avoid looking awkwardly at odds with him in the eye of the public.

'Oh my god, I'm sorry to hear this. I mean how are you are taking all of this?' Molly asked, gently stroking Tin's shoulder as her way of expressing empathy.

'I was surprised initially but now I'm kind of numb. I don't exactly know where to go from here,' Tin whispered.

A few women sitting diagonally across from them were laughing so loudly and merrily that Tin could not help but allow the pseudo-festive aura to mute her negative sentiment for a fractional moment.

'What do you mean you don't exactly know? It all boils down to whether you still want to go out with him or not,' Molly spoke in a tone more concerned than confrontational.

'That's the thing, I don't know,' Tin muttered without taking her gaze off the distant trees beyond the field.

Molly leaned towards Tin and embraced her from the side with both arms. Against the sharp bones of Molly's shoulder, Tin rested her head. They stayed silent for a while until Tin decided to perk up and say, 'By the way, do you think they have a clue about their mother's daily whereabouts? I mean, do you know what she does for a living?'

'Well, you should probably be aware by now that secrets don't exactly stay secret in this village,' Molly replied.

According to her, Chew Yong had been aware of his mother's work for quite a while now. He merely pretended he knew nothing when she was around him and he confessed to Molly that he was beyond caring what others thought of her, secure in the knowledge that his mum had no choice but to make a hard decision for the sake of survival after the passing of her husband, his father. Not only could he empathize, he was more bent than ever to excel in his studies and hopefully get a job that pays well to buy her manumission from the daily humiliation and scorn associated with her kind of job and to ensure Ming Hao, who also happened to know the means with which their mother had been supporting the family, finish his studies without having to be weighed down by money issues.

'So, Ming Hao knows?' asked Tin.

Molly nodded. She then talked about her evening with Chew Yong, the rides, her take on his personality ('Sometimes I can just throttle him for being too optimistic and believing everything will work out fine!'), dribs and drabs of their conversation leading up to that final proposal.

'What? Are you serious?' Tin straightened her posture, her face lit up in disbelief, matching in spirit the onslaught of fireflies swirling around them.

Molly nodded, this time biting her nether lip in a show of playful indecisiveness while twirling a lock of her hair.

'Wow, I'm so happy for you,' Tin exclaimed, taking Molly's hands in hers and ecstatically flipping them up and down before being nudged to calm down with a counter-flip.

'I have not said yes,' Molly interrupted. There was an unsettling quality to the way she spoke: it was both guarded and confiding at once. 'But I have to let him know soon. He's leaving Singapore in a few weeks' time.'

The fireflies continued to make their presence felt, setting a portion of the field aglow, making the people sitting around and having their tête-à-têtes breathe the air of these moments of uplift when the personal fell away, and with it, the usual fears and worries.

Chapter Ten

'Uncle Ah Poong Nair is here, he's here!' shouted the children, one after another, who had been hunting for scorpions in the open field and crushing them with their mallets, a favourite pastime of children growing up in Lorong Limau especially when the weather was hot and muggy with scorpions emerging in abundance from their nests. They called him Ah Poong Nair, a colloquial sobriquet for Indians, at once derogatory and droll depending on which half of the scale it was tipping over; he was the barber who would pay house visits at least once a month in each village to provide haircut services to exclusively men of all ages from babies to geriatrics with each haircut costing thirty cents (women, on the other hand, would help cut each other's hair; of course the wealthier ones would have it done in the salons).

The children ran towards him, flouncing around this bony man dressed in an oversized button-down purple shirt and a pair of deep khaki shorts as if he were a famous celebrity. His eyeballs were disproportionately white, and he had an air of alacrity about him; he also had the habit of breathing through his mouth due to a chronically blocked nose, no thanks to the ills of his profession causing him to inhale minuscule hair together with all its toxicity for the longest time. To keep that at bay, it was believed that barbers must make it a point to overdose on the consumption of radish. Only a diet rich in radish, based on an old wives' tale, would clear the toxicity in the nasal passage.

He seemed to enthral the kids more than anyone else, driven in equal parts by where he originally came from (South India) and what he did for a living (one of the only two foreign barbers around). They tried to make him laugh—which he often did unless he was on a time crunch—by rendering all kinds of funny faces, mouths outstretched, eyebrows arched dramatically, a means to get his attention. And as he traipsed to the spot where he would deliver his service, the common water point in the case of Lorong Limau, he could be sure the children would be right behind him like an audience bewitched by a sorcerer.

Less fanatical but just as loyal was his other audience: the paying customers. At the sound of the children's siren call, they would make a beeline for the water point. The first man in the queue would sit on the chair provided by Jude Vincent, take off his top, and patiently wait for the barber. This morning, that first person happened to be Ah Fook, the teenage son of a carpenter living a few units away from Mona.

In less than ten minutes, the barber arrived at the water-point. The children continued to faff around but the moment he retrieved a pair of scissors and a comb from his black rubber bag and worked his craft, they immediately stopped their nonsense and began studying him in silent wonder.

Before long, the snipping and shearing were accompanied by half-suppressed laughter and amused countenances from the other men awaiting their haircut as they watched the barber unflinchingly tilt the head of Ah Fook in various untoward angles.

Gau Pee happened to walk past the men in the queue on her way to Mona's place, feeling reasonably peeved that no one even attempted to whistle at her out of flirtation. Instead, they looked away, preferring to focus their attention on the barber. If she were Molly or some other pretty girl, she knew the men would have teasingly hollered: 'Wanna go out with me?' or 'Hey beautiful!' Acknowledging that in the privacy of her thought, she allowed a flicker of annoyance to pass over her face. *Never mind*, she told herself, *I will work on Chew Yong who's far more educated and better-looking than any of these losers.*

She was bent on only one thing: smearing Molly's reputation in front of Mona which would leave the latter not much of a choice but to compel her son Chew Yong to break up with Molly, after which, she could have him all for herself. The very thought unleashed a trill of a laugh from her as she approached Mona's unit—three blocks away from hers—on a Tuesday morning, apparently Mona's off-day in the week according to what she had learnt from her inquiry at Glorious Hole Hotel.

Her unannounced visit caught Mona by surprise. She had no idea Gau Pee should have been taken seriously when she had said she would pay her a visit in the near future during their brief encounter outside the army barracks; she thought it was a mere pleasantry. Most of all, she could not fathom why Gau Pee suddenly wanted to get close to her after sullying her reputation in the village with all that name-calling: slut, whore, tramp.

'Oh, Aunty Mona, I'm so happy to see you again,' Gau Pee exclaimed when Mona opened the door to her unit. 'You do remember me, don't you? I'm a good friend of Chew Yong.'

'Uh, I . . . I think . . .' Mona was left searching for words, overwhelmed in part by the over-the-top greeting and in part by that unmistakable nose up close.

'Can I come in?' Gau Pee remained in her zealous mode.

'Uh, I'm sorry, can we perhaps chat outside the house? My mother-in-law is napping at the moment,' Mona whispered, hoping Gau Pee would get the drift that she seriously needed to tone down her voice.

She ushered her uninvited guest to a pair of weather-beaten lawn chairs in front of her unit, both sitting down at the same time. Gau Pee began by propitiating her reluctant host with smarmy remarks: 'Oh you look so young and pretty', 'I really admire you for raising two sons on your own and taking care of your mother-in-law at the same time', 'Chew Yong is so lucky to have a selfless mum like you.' However, sensing that Mona was ill at ease with her compliments, she wasted no time to execute her main strategy, telling her how worried she had been for Chew Yong after finding out that he had been dating Molly, 'her neighbour of dubious reputation'. She lied to Mona about Molly's broken month status ('Chew Yong might suffer dire consequences if he were to marry her') and that she'd had sex with every man on her matchmaking list and subsequently refused to marry them.

'Haven't you heard? She even had Mr Tang eating out of her hand,' said Gau Pee in a display of faux coyness. Mr Tang was of course one of the most well-known business tycoons in Singapore, mega-rich, reportedly smitten with Molly after spotting her at the market and thereafter aiming to make her his wife. It was true that Molly had met up with Mr Tang in a matchmaking arrangement, and despite her outrageous antics, the likes of nose-picking and eye-twitching, Mr Tang simply could not let her go and kept pestering the matchmaker to seal the deal.

'She's probably the village's biggest slut!' said Gau Pee with the most reaffirming, reckless smile. In response, Mona stared hard at the bunch of men queuing up for their haircut in the distance, paralysed by embarrassment at having to listen to one villager cast aspersions on another. Gau Pee on the other hand was expecting her to at least nod in agreement and perhaps say out loud about warning her son against dating such a girl. But no, nothing, not a word or sign of acquiescence, Mona's reticence on the subject echoing its awkward quiet in Gau Pee's gossip-dinned ears.

Desperate for some form of consort, Gau Pee tore into the jugular. 'Aren't you worried that Chew Yong is seeing someone who only knows how to spread her legs for boys?' But something caught like a fish bone in her throat as soon as she said it. How could she have been so oblivious talking about loose morals and sluttiness to one who happened to be working in the sex industry? It would be a miracle if Mona had not found the talk offensive. Realizing she might have committed a boo-boo, she reined in her judgemental persona and started delving into how much she truly cared for Chew Yong in a rare display of demureness.

'If Chew Yong were to become my husband, I promise to support and serve him till the end of days, you can be sure of that,' she giggled, palm covering her mouth in mild embarrassment.

Still, Mona remained moored to her gut feeling. That Gau Pee had been repeatedly maligning her in the village was so firmly burnt into her memory that now it was difficult for her to see this gossipy woman in a new light. For the next ten minutes as Gau Pee nattered on about what a perfect fit she would be for Chew Yong, Mona merely offered herself as an unwilling listener. After a while, Gau Pee could finally see through Mona's intentions, dropping hints here and there—looking at passers-by, twirling her hair distractedly— that she just about had enough of this one-way conversation, that Gau Pee's past misdeeds could never be expiated with repeat blandishments ('You must tell me your secret to staying young and beautiful.') But since Gau Pee appeared determined to continue talking, Mona decided to interrupt, saying something in the context of checking on her mother- in-law who might need some sort of assistance to go to the toilet and thanking Gau Pee for dropping by, perfectly polite but in such a way that her guest would realize the time was getting on and would have no choice but to rise to her feet and bid goodbye, a rather disgruntled goodbye in her case.

While it might have taken Mona quite a while to finally get Gau Pee off her back, it did not take her long to gain the trust of the skinny girl working at Glorious Hole. Over the last few weeks, they had been spending much time together on and off work. At the brothel, when they were not serving clients, they would sneak into the courtyard away from the glare of the matron to mostly have a lengthy heart-to-heart. On their off days, Mona would invite the skinny girl to her place for a cup of coffee or tea; sometimes they would window-shop in Chinatown, admiring everything from diamonds and pearls, which Mona had been able to afford prior to the passing of her husband, to specialty food items like ancient herbs and red bean cakes. As it turned out, the skinny girl had grown to regard Mona as a mother, having been an orphan all her life. In fact, she had become the only friend of Mona since the latter's move to Lorong Limau, as most of the other villagers tended to shun her due to her line of work and her old friends, the wealthy women of leisure, had abandoned her. Of course, there was also Jim Vincent but she saw him more as a makeshift boss and an authority figure rather than a friend or even a friendly acquaintance. Although he had been surreptitiously paying her for her investigative work at Glorious Hole, presumably out of his own pocket, she knew their pact would probably have to be terminated sooner or later if she still could not ferret out any evidence pertaining to Ah Hock's mysterious demise.

'I'll give you two to three more weeks at most but if it's still coming up blank then you're on your own. You can either choose to continue working in the brothel or go back to your free-agent days, I don't really care.' Jim Vincent had served her the warning a few days following Gau Pee's unexpected drop-in at her place. After hearing what he had to say, one would expect Mona to feel either relieved (no more snooping around behind the matron's back) or pressurized (she had to uncover the truth in no time). However, she was anything but. Instead, she felt a little let down although it was not clear whether it was the loss of a confirmed source of income or his impending absence in her life that was making her feel the way she was. Sure, the monthly stipend was instrumental to alleviating some of her family expenses; sure, she did get the vibe from Jim Vincent that he cared for her to a certain extent. After all, he had let her escape during the raid on the ship. 'I don't really care.' Those very words more or less stabbed her in the front.

One afternoon at the brothel, she decided to shift gears, rather bent on obtaining information that would at least be substantial enough for Jim Vincent to close the case of Ah Hock. It was high time, she told herself, to grasp the nettle. After her session with a client, she approached the skinny girl, grabbed her by her arm, and started sobbing as if she were experiencing a mental breakdown. She kept repeating, 'I can't take this any more . . . the guy almost died on me,' her body convulsing in a wave of spasms. The skinny girl tried to calm her down by leading her to a chair in the pantry and making her a cup of hot tea.

'What happened? Were you abused or violated in any way?' asked the skinny girl.

'No, I was so scared . . . he almost died of a heart attack when we were doing it,' said a hyperventilating Mona who surprised herself that she could pull off something of this nature rather convincingly. 'I wouldn't know what to do had he really died . . . this is way too much for me to handle. I mean, would the police have believed me at all if it'd truly happened?' She continued to follow her thespian instinct, crying, mumbling incoherently.

At first the skinny girl merely listened, uttering not a word. Then, as Mona had envisaged, it all came out, unbridled. Once she got started it was like she could not stop, like the only thing was to keep talking and talking, like some bee buzzing in the bonnet. She rushed headlong into the matter of Ah Hock, how he had collapsed in a drugged state and how the matron had arranged for him to be driven to some faraway place and dropped off without even finding out whether he was alive or not. She added that she had been crippled by guilt all this while especially with the matron breathing down her neck and forbidding anyone involved to ever talk about what had happened.

Without revealing she was working undercover for Jim Vincent, Mona encouraged the skinny girl to confess to the police so that she would not be implicated once the truth came to light.

'You will go to prison if you don't confess, that's something I'm sure of,' said Mona, now free of her actress-like demeanour. In the end, she was surprised that she faced not much of a resistance in the process of getting the skinny girl to talk to Jim Vincent, 'her friend from the police'.

Within days of her confession, the Glorious Hole was permanently shut down by Jim and his team. The infamous Looi family, owner of the brothel, had their license revoked; the matron got what she deserved: a two-year prison term for the obstruction of a police investigation; the skinny girl was spared any form of chastisement owing to her disclosure of pertinent evidence; the rest, namely the driver and the other two prostitutes, were merely issued a stern warning.

The shutdown of the brothel left many of its regular patrons frustrated, their endowments practically hanging unsated between the legs. As a result, freelance workers like Mona suddenly found their appointment calendars booked to the hilt until the next brothel came onto the scene two years thereafter. But she decided not to take advantage of it, instead quietly withdrawing from the industry upon Chew Yong's graduation and trying her hand at acting. Later, she went on to become a household name on television, acting in many local dramas usually playing the role she had once been so familiar with in real life: a wealthy housewife.

Chapter Eleven

'Gan-ni-na, who the hell gives you the permission to go dating before your older sister is even married?' Tin's father shouted at his third daughter who happened to be clearing the dinner table after he and Bok Koon—the remaining men in the family—had had their meals. Everyone present was taken aback to hear that favourite expletive of his, largely absent from his parlance since Ah Hock's death.

Apparently, Gau Pee had earlier told her parents that Tin was seeing a boy by the name of Ming Hao, certain that their reaction would be a unified steadfast 'no', since parents of that generation would rarely permit any daughter (Tin) to bypass matchmaking let alone go steady with a boy before the older one (Gau Pee) got married. Gau Pee's customary sneer curled the left side of her lower lip as she watched her sister being taunted by their father.

'You're insensible! Can't you exercise a bit of patience and wait for your sister to get hitched before you even think about going on dates? I don't understand why you're in such a hurry to have a boyfriend. No, let me rephrase that: I expect you to pick your future husband through matchmaking, only though matchmaking and nothing else!' Tin's mother added with unequivocal disapproval.

'What if she never gets married?' Kee Kee asked in half-jest. 'Does it mean Tin and I will forever not be allowed to get married? What will happen to the prince of my dreams?'

'You shut your trap, gan-ni-na! We're not talking about you here,' Tin's father let out his habitual yell.

Gau Pee shot Kee Kee a nasty, piercing look till the latter started to visibly shake in fear. Her tacit message to her younger sibling: *Beware, I will deal with you later.* 'Who says Gau Pee will never get married? Any guy will be lucky to have her as his wife,' said Tin's mother. To the uninitiated, it would appear that she might truly be blindsided by blood relations so much so she could not even admit the hideousness of her daughter's facial structure.

Tin remained quiet in the face of parental opposition. She knew better than to reason with them. Deep down inside, she had already made up her mind to continue seeing Ming Hao on the sly despite his inexplicable resistance while assuring her parents she would break off with him, a demand they were bound to impose on her in order for the family to move past this matter.

What did complicate things further was that Tin's mother had already targeted someone else to be her future husband, thanks to Sweet Shirley's recommendation. Once Gau Pee managed to secure her matrimonial union, which only Tin's mother and Gau Pee and no one else had the confidence would eventually materialize, Tin was expected to throw herself into the arms of this person whom her mother had in mind. He was known as Ah Sokh, the chief warden of

Singapore Outram Prison, a man who had achieved his own success by dint of hard work and persistence. Already married with two wives and eight children and notably three decades older than Tin, Ah Sokh was not exactly shopping for a third wife until he was convinced by Sweet Shirley the matchmaker that a younger companion would help him ward off dotage by adding some spice to his life, so he thought to himself why not give it a shot.

He had earlier visited Tin's household to meet up with Gau Pee, Sweet Shirley's original pick, and was about to run for the hills as expected but found himself enthralled by Tin who happened to walk to the kitchen past the living room where he, Tin's mother, Gau Pee, and Sweet Shirley were present. After the meeting, he indicated to Sweet Shirley that he was rather keen to make Tin his third wife. Sweet Shirley subsequently conveyed Ah Sokh's proposal to Tin's mother who was more than happy to oblige based on two conditions: they would not disclose their pact to Gau Pee for fear she might get hurt, and Tin could only get married after Gau Pee had done so.

'I think Ming Hao's not right for you,' Bok Koon, the introvert in the family, muttered out of nowhere, not looking at anyone in particular. He gave off the glazed vibe of a tired army personnel like he had been digging trenches into the night. They all craned their heads in his direction, simultaneously surprised and alarmed by his monotone parenthesis. Tin felt more hurt and betrayed than taken aback by Bok Koon's sudden unexpected cavil. She failed to understand how someone to whom she was closest in the family, someone on whom she had been showering her emotional support, could have turned against her without finding out the head or tail of the matter.

'What do you mean by that?' Tin asked, no longer able to restrain herself.

Bok Koon neither responded nor looked at her; he simply made his way to the bedroom he once shared with Ah Hock and remained there till everyone retreated from the discussion much later in the evening. But then again, Bok Koon had always been a connoisseur of pessimism and despair.

'You see, even your dumb brother agrees with us,' said Tin's father. 'You'd better break off with him or I'll break your leg, gan-ni-na!'

'Pa, don't worry. I can tell the boy is not even interested in her. It's all one-sided,' Gau Pee interjected, grinning like one of those villains featured in the early Cantonese kung fu movies of that era.

At that point, Tin fired off her salvo ad lib. 'At least Ming Hao agrees to go out with me even though he's not exactly my boyfriend yet. What about yourself? You've never even gone on a date with Chew Yong for all I know. He's madly in love with Molly and not you, so who's being one-sided now?'

In a withering response, Gau Pee slapped Tin on her face, hard and resolute. Goaded by their parents who insisted that Tin should never ever have behaved this rudely with her older sister, Gau Pee slapped Tin once again, this time even more forcefully than before.

Molly's mother and Mona spoke for the first time even though they had seen each other quite a bit in the village. The mood was cordial. It was a get-together initiated by Chew Yong in his house. Apart from the soon-to-wed and their mothers, Ming Hao was also in attendance. First came the pleasantries

('I like your samfu' or 'The weather's getting better') followed by the usual small talk apropos Lorong Limau—which seller offered the best fish or vegetables in the market, which seamstress provided value-for-money clothes and so forth. Shortly after, Chew Yong and Molly officially sought the consent of their respective mothers seated next to each other, kneeling down in front of them at their feet.

Molly's mother felt relieved when Mona told everyone present that she would be leaving her 'current job' for acting opportunities in the local if not regional market. With the elephant in the room having been addressed and the official wedding proposal accepted by both matriarchs, everyone started conversing with one another in the most natural manner except Ming Hao who stuck to his usual conduct: reserved, distant, locking whatever inner life he might have behind an aloof, unfailingly polite demeanour, the awkwardness of which Molly attempted to dispel.

'Hey Ming Hao, I heard from Tin that you like to swim in the open seas. I mean that sounds kind of dangerous, doesn't it?' asked a chirpy Molly with an equally cheerful Chew Yong watching her fondly as one might a beloved child, while Mona and Molly's mother appeared to be engaged in a rather intimate dialogue on World War II.

Ming Hao merely shrugged his shoulders and excused himself, saying he had an appointment to keep; he picked up presumably his satchel from a nearby chair and left the house as quietly as he had owned his presence earlier when his brother and Molly were seeking formal consent for their marriage.

After Ming Hao's departure, Molly whispered to Chew Yong, 'Did I say something wrong? He didn't appear too pleased as far as I can see.'

'Ugh, just ignore him. He's been experiencing mood swings for the longest time ever. Sometimes he's smiling to himself, other times he goes through the day without even saying a word. It's hard to figure him out and honestly speaking, I've kind of given up trying,' replied Chew Yong with a tinge of exasperation.

'I know he's an introvert but goodness, are you telling me he's been like that since he was young?'

'Yeah, pretty much so.'

'Gosh, I was merely making conversation, yet he seemed not in the least interested like I was Medusa or someone about to put a curse on him,' said Molly with affected insouciance.

'I know he can be exasperating but he's my younger brother after all so please forgive him with all your heart.' Chew Yong pleaded playfully.

'Not to worry, my heart can't say no to you,' Molly giggled, gently placing her hand on his thigh.

While Chew Yong and Molly were busy making wedding plans, Tin and Ming Hao appeared to be stuck in their own inertia, at times even slipping a few notches down from status quo, not that it had been a sizzling hotbed of romance to begin with. To any punctilious observer, it would appear as if they were conducting themselves on radically different tangents. Tin was always the one asking Ming Hao out; she was always trying to get him on a conversational path but his voice would choke with inarticulate agony if he spoke for more than a minute; she sought shelter in his eyes but he simply returned an empty gaze; she had even, on one of those occasions, steeled her nerves and kissed him on the lips despite knowing that the act itself would be frowned upon by society at large as rather unbecoming of a lady and despite going against the very nature of her public decorum. If the reciprocating kiss had turned out to be exemplary, it would have at least been worth the risk taken. Sadly, his kiss felt more dutiful than impassioned. On the whole, he seemed to emanate that Kafkaesque vibe of never being sure. If nothing else, he reminded her of her youngest brother Bok Koon, the kind of guys who were born without the extrovert gene, inadequate for socializing in public.

Sometimes, they would spend an afternoon walking side by side on the beach, the closest their bodies would be since the time she planted that one and only kiss on him, each careful not to touch the other, and sometimes they would end up in the neighbourhood sitting by the river, watching children catch spiders or play catch, struggling to overcome the awkwardness caused by his reticence, a mot juste Tin would often use to describe to Molly his less than clear-cut feelings towards her, aware that she could not explain it without making it sound like more than it was.

'Perhaps he's just shy, or perhaps he's showing you respect by not doing anything untoward or improper,' said Molly who tried to comfort her best friend.

But, as she had also related to Molly, there was one thing that she did pick up from their interaction, something simultaneously inexplicable and blatant—sweat stains peppering his shirt as well as underneath his armpits. Each time he showed up, invariably late, no matter what the weather—warm, windy, clear skies—it would appear he simply had no control over his sweat glands. Granted Ming Hao was pudgy and might sweat a little more, it still made no sense to her especially when she knew he would hardly quicken his pace let alone run each time he was late for their appointment. More often than not, he would saunter up to her in the most casual of manners and apologize for being tardy. Nothing more, nothing less. Of course, she would eventually figure out in the near future the reason behind all that excessive sweating: heading from some covert rendezvous to their date could undoubtedly work up a sweat.

Tin would also notice the anxious, fatalistic quality of his eyes each time he spoke like he was about to make a dreadful confession. At some bleary point, he would be tongue-tied and completely at sea, a few words spoken nonetheless, leaving Tin equally if not more uncomfortable. There were a couple of times she did attempt to drop hints of her genuine affection for him—a gentle brush of her shoulder against his, sharing with him a secret that she vowed she had never told anyone, smiling at him in a way that most would associate with either a state of infatuation or deteriorating mental health—so much so that he recoiled like a dog being physically taunted by its abuser. Unable to dislodge the chill between Ming Hao and her after going on several dates, Tin already knew in her heart of hearts, but was afraid to admit openly, that her relationship with him might be similar to Gau Pee's with Chew Yong, one-sided as always. But she was not ready to give up just yet; she planned to have a brutally honest talk with him soon. *Perhaps he's already seeing another girl, or maybe he's preoccupied with matters that he simply can't share with me,* Tin ruminated. However, what was to follow would leach the life out of her in aspects impossible to repair.

Chapter Twelve

Gau Pee heard everything she would rather not hear about Chew Yong's wedding proposal to Molly. In Lorong Limau, news as such could not be kept under wraps for long, usually not more than an hour depending on the significance of the story and the eagerness of the villagers to propagate it. 'The wedding would reportedly take place in two weeks' time', 'Both families had given their consent', 'Chew Yong and Molly must be in bliss now'—it was like a dream to her where the details became fainter the harder you tried to grasp them. The air around her was suddenly too stale to breathe, the exact suffocating feeling of being left behind in the parade far too many times.

How could she have not suspected something was afoot? She should have caught a whiff of it during her recent encounter with Molly at the common corridor shared by both their families. As usual, Gau Pee had been taking diabolical delight in taunting Molly.

'I hear some sailors are in town. Looks like you're all dressed up to throw yourself at them?' Gau Pee had said, accompanied by a laughter that was thick and full of educated malice.

Instead of hitting back with some choice words of her own, as she would normally do in past scenarios, Molly had simply smiled, not the sarcastic I'm-going-to-get-you but the holding-out-an-olive-branch kind of smile. In a rare burst of adversarial graciousness, she said, 'I really don't wish to fight with you any more, and I just want you to be happy.'

'Huh! Has the world gone mad or is it just you?' Gau Pee had snapped at Molly, regarding her with disdain as would a meat lover a bowl of vegetables.

Thinking back, it should have raised some bells and whistles in her mind, as Molly simply would not have reacted with such benevolence after getting insulted for no reason unless she had been harbouring a piece of joyful news which in this case happened to be her imminent wedding.

She vowed to stop the wedding no matter what, even if it meant finding untapped pockets of sordidness inside her already crowded palette of weaponry to break up the couple. Right now, the plan was to head to Chew Yong's place to exact a smear campaign against his bride-to-be but first she would have to conspire with a few guys who owed her favours because of her past actions—letting them jump queue at the water point or getting Jude Vincent to help them find work—to raise a collective voice detailing how and when Molly had had an orgy with them not just once but a couple of times. If that could not rankle Chew Yong even for a bit, she was not sure what else would, knowing any decent man would demand a morally upright if not chaste woman for his wife.

After coercing the guys—five of them to be exact—to spin their unified story of orgies with Molly with eidetic narrative imperatives like what had led them to her, the venue, date and time, coital revelations, even down to what they were wearing on that day and who said what, she warned them about Chew Yong probably approaching some if not all of them to want to verify the truth and advised them to 'act as normal as possible'. With the plan laid out clearly, she walked over to Chew Yong's place all ready to *unleash her concern for him after learning that he and Molly were about to get married* (her prevailing thought bubble).

Just as she was about to knock on his door, she heard some kind of noise coming from inside. It sounded like a whispery dialogue peppered with mild laughter, the kind you would associate with flirtation or even erotic seduction. At this, Gau Pee's heart skipped a beat, fairly sure Chew Yong and Molly must be engaging in sex. *But what about his house-ridden grandmother, the one who's blind and possibly half-deaf at her age? They wouldn't dare take the risk with her around even if Mona and Ming Hao were out of the house. Or did Mona happen to bring her mother-in-law out for a walk to help her escape the drabness of being stuck inside the house every single day?* All these thoughts drifted in and out of her mind while she made her way to a side window facing the courtyard so that she could take a peek at what was going on inside the house.

It was exactly the same scene Tin had witnessed a day earlier—the same place, the same time—when she decided to pay Ming Hao a surprise visit only to find herself piqued by the same surreptitious mix of dialogue and laughter her sister was now trying to verify.

Momentarily shocked, Tin could not wrap her mind around what she saw, utterly confused to discover the iniquity of a world people could find themselves in, beholding which she felt repulsed beyond words, acknowledging that days like this when the margin between perception and reality stood not like a line drawn in the sand but like an uncharted ravine. At the same time, she felt something revelatory cohering in hindsight, all the tell tale signs, the shyness, the laconic impressions, the perspiration, the waffling, the distractions. In her village where so many young boys seemed like anagrams of one another—playing football, catching spiders, talking aloud—a few like Ming Hao stood out rather distinctly. Only a last scrap of self-preservation kept her from fainting on the spot.

Not unlike Tin, Gau Pee felt wobbly upon witnessing what she just had, except minutes thereafter, she happily realized it might just be the perfect foil to a wedding because no one worth his salt would get married in the wake of a familial scandal. As expected, it made no difference to her whatsoever that her younger brother was going to be part of this scandal as long as she could throw a monkey wrench into Chew Yong's and Molly's imminent wedding.

There they were, with seldom-seen, unrestrained smiles. It was an improbable affection that must have surmounted society's gravest taboos on the way to a bittersweet consummation. Their whole demeanours shifted away from the reticent, guarded teenagers they usually appeared to be towards the loving, free-spirited individuals many would not have thought they were.

Ming Hao and Bok Koon were busy engorging themselves with kisses while standing up, their half-naked bodies pressed together. Those who knew these boys for a long time would have been coerced into imagining let alone believing the scene played out in front of Gau Pee: the way Ming Hao's eyes kept searching his paramour's, and Bok Koon's his, and how each caressed and lingered on the other's gaze.

Unbelievable! Gau Pee thought to herself with a conniving smile triggered by what was already germinating in her mind to wreck her nemesis' wedding. But for Tin, it must have been traumatic to watch, even for a few seconds, the indignities of a relationship wherein she had felt seduced by the romance of it, wholly self-constructed to begin with, energized by its possibilities which practically went nowhere, and the equally harsh pain of seeing a potential husband, at least from her viewpoint, slowly fade into someone else's arms, that of her younger brother.

Under the strain of her discovery, Tin had walked away from Mona's shack to the far end of the field in Lorong Limau, every step taken by her seemed too heavy for her own gait. She had sat down on the grass, thinking about how to face Ming Hao as well as her brother in the days that followed, equal parts leery of telling the truth and afraid to concoct a lie that would only make her feel more unsettled than she already was. After some rumination, she came to the understanding that much of what was to be said did not matter at all, and that much of what mattered could never be said.

Gau Pee, on the other hand, ran as fast as she could after her discovery to the police station next to the bus terminal and managed to convince two policemen to follow her to Mona's place to verify her report on an illegal sexual union. True to her claim, the policemen found two unchaste guys in a mortise and tenon alliance.

In Mona's household, it was nothing short of chaos. She almost went off the rails after being informed by the police that her youngest son had been arrested for 'an illegal act', yelping and banging her forehead repeatedly against the wall, only to be pried away from injuring herself any further by Chew Yong who was very much beside himself, confused, helpless, angry with whoever had instigated the arrest. Only Mona's blind mother-in-law appeared to be kept in the dark due to her being hard of hearing despite the commotion taking place around her.

In what seemed like a turnaround in her reaction, Mona decided to stop all her crying and departed along with Chew Yong to the police station looking for Jim Vincent, the person who had once spared her from incarceration, hoping he could help her again this time round, perhaps to mitigate the charge against Ming Hao with the plausible reason that her son might not even have realized he'd done something illegal in the first place.

'I'd actually meant to pay you a visit later today,' said Jim Vincent when confronted by a teary Mona and Chew Yong at the station.

'Please help me, please, please, I beg of you,' pleaded Mona, holding Jim Vincent's arm with both hands.

'I'm sorry, there's really nothing much I can do . . . it's an undisputed law and nobody, not even I can challenge it,' he explained. However, she continued to plead for clemency, breaking down into hysterics. All he could offer was a long, tight embrace which frankly made her feel slightly better at least for those few minutes their bodies were held together.

Over at Tin's household, the mood was grim although what would appear like sombreness from afar was revealed at close range to be impregnable devastation. Tin's father had earlier stormed out of the house while sputtering gan-ni-na non-stop upon receiving the news from two policemen at his doorstep; Tin's mother became faint-hearted and collapsed, hitting her butt hard on the cement floor. Gau Pee and Tin lifted her up and sat her on a chair, breathing words of comfort into her ears—'He'll fine, it's not so bad, they'll probably let him off the hook'—even though they hardly believed any of it; neither Tin nor her mother knew Gau Pee was merely putting on a show of fake empathy. After a while, when she was more collected, Tin's mother instructed her daughters to remain at home and left the house to visit her son who had been held in custody at the police station since his arrest.

Given what had happened to Ah Hock and now that Bok Koon was in a situation of possibly the most shameful order, not to mention the years of having to give up some of her infant daughters for adoption, it would take a long time for Tin's mother to reclaim her well-being, as she had drawn too deeply upon subterranean reservoirs of her resilience that, once tapped, might never be replenished by therapy and recuperation.

Like her mother, Kee Kee initially felt a stab of nausea—'morally corrupt', 'illegal', 'obscene' were words spoken by the police which she deemed too heavy for her soft feet that morning—but bounced back rather quickly on her own terms, retreated to the boys' bedroom (since the girls had no bedroom of their own and slept on mattresses in the living room), and prayed hard that she would one day marry a prince who would then offer a royal pardon for her brother.

'A crime involving unnatural sex,' primarily the message delivered by the police, spoken with slow, accusatory restraint, played over and over in the head of what appeared to be a coma-bound Tin, countering her will to banish the very image of Ming Hao, her supposed romantic interest, together with Bok Koon, the only sibling who was close to her, persisting in her mind with a full measure of lucidity. In fact, the pangs caused by the image seemed to have metastasized to other parts of her body if that was even possible, her skin aflame with perspiratory distress, hands trembling from time to time. She mostly kept her head down and hastened her breathing as though it would help stave off the truth of the matter.

All this time, Gau Pee was the only one who did not seem as vexed as the rest; even her pretence of empathy towards her mother was as disposable as melted ice. Knowing that Tin was deep in agony, instead of putting family welfare ahead of personal vendetta, she took the opportunity to chafe her sister.

'Ha, isn't it ironic that the person who once said that I'd been indulging in a one-sided relationship is now living her own accusation? Guess who's having the last laugh now?' Gau Pee said, every syllable spiked with a juxtaposition of venom and contemptuous amusement.

Tin raised her head in acknowledgement, too emotionally bludgeoned to deconstruct that loaded remark.

'So how does it feel? Painful? Hurt? Ha, I think you deserve every bit of it!' Gau Pee happily uttered.

Tin merely looked at her sister in a sort of vacant way, by now grasping what she was driving at. Not wanting to start a verbal feud, Tin mumbled, 'I'm going to start preparing lunch for today.' As she was about to walk off to the kitchen Gau Pee grabbed her by the shoulder and forced her to turn around, obviously not done with her taunting.

'You're partly responsible for what has happened, do you know that?'

'I don't know what you're saying,' Tin replied softly, dazed, apparently disconnected.

'You don't know? Really? What a joke!' Gau Pee retorted. 'All this wouldn't have taken place if you would have had Ming Hao under control. Obviously, you're not good enough for him, that's why he has to go and seduce our younger brother.'

The accusation jolted Tin from her slumber but she appeared ruminant, not yet given to any hasty rebuttal.

'Nothing to say? Guilty as charged?' Gau Pee said, hands on her hips, a deadly smirk on her face.

'Look, I really don't wish to get into this right now,' Tin said. 'I think I'd better start cooking. Ma and Pa will be back later and I'm sure they will be famished.'

'Ming Hao, Ming Hao, Ming Hao . . . who would have thought he'll ditch you for a guy?' Gau Pee said with a touch of relish.

'Look, our brother is probably suffering right now so I think we should be pulling our resources together to find out how to get him out of jail rather than talk about me and Ming Hao,' Tin said, neither emphatic nor feeble in tone.

'Ha, if you truly care for Bok Koon, you wouldn't have allowed Ming Hao to stray and then seduce our brother into doing something illegal, it's all your fault,' Gau Pee said. 'Oh wait, maybe it's because he finds you totally unattractive and you've caused him to give up on women altogether.'

'This is not fair. You're just being vindictive,' Tin murmured calmly.

'How dare you,' Gau Pee slapped her younger sister without hesitation.

Tin remained largely unaffected, as it was not the first time she had been slapped by Gau Pee for remotely standing up to her.

'Let me also tell you this. It's not just Ming Hao that you've driven into committing this immoral crime but also Bok Koon because he's closest to you and he must have developed his aversion to women in general after spending all that time with you, a tomboy at heart, who's clueless about using your feminine assets to attract guys.'

Tin stared hard at Gau Pee, nostrils tightening in anger.

'On the contrary, I think he has been observing *you* for the longest time and must have realized how vindictive you are and think all women are like that so it's just as easy for me to put the blame on you,' Tin fired back, raising her voice just a little.

Gau Pee slapped Tin yet again, this time harder than the last. Kee Kee heard all this in the boys' bedroom but knew better than to emerge from hiding to try to help her sisters make peace with each other for fear she might be slapped by Gau Pee in no time, which was the last thing she wanted: invoke the bastardization of her status as a future princess.

'Say that again? Say it! I dare you!' Gau Pee challenged Tin to further provoke her.

In retrospect, what followed was a preview of Tin's indomitable spirit as she began to develop roles that would define her adulthood: a woman with an ironclad will to overcome pain, a martyr, a punctilious caregiver, one who saw her needs as nugatory compared to that of her loved ones.

'I will go and prepare the food now,' Tin said as if she were issuing an instruction, reining in whatever hurt she was feeling.

'Go! Get out of my sight,' Gau Pee uttered in disgust. 'You've wasted enough of my time when I could be comforting Chew Yong right now. Ha, after all, I wouldn't have reported the case to the police if I didn't think there's nothing for me to gain here.'

It was a slip of the tongue. She had no intention of revealing the truth, but she blurted out inadvertently. Now she had no choice other than to buttress her line of reasoning.

Tin froze midway through her amble to the kitchen, turned back and confronted Gau Pee. 'What do you mean you reported the case to the police?'

She glared at her older sister. Gau Pee glared back with a menacing look. Tin met her eyes fearlessly.

'Why can't I do it? Is it wrong to want to protect Chew Yong from that bitch of a neighbour, your so-called best friend? I figure this is the only way to stop his wedding, to prevent him from making a lifelong mistake. He should be thanking me instead,' Gau Pee said, her left fist balling up in vehemence.

By now, Tin's moral outrage was too great for her not to respond to Gau Pee in the most deserving outcome. She did not so much return her sister's impenitence as toss it back like a live grenade, slapping her on the face not just once but three times in a row.

'You selfish, heartless idiot! How can you send our brother to jail for your own benefit? Aren't you even human at all?' Tin lambasted her like never before.

However, Gau Pee was not one to wince from intimidation let alone getting slapped. Flying into a blasting fury, she picked up a broom lying nearby and whipped Tin repeatedly till the latter sustained blotches of vermilion on her body.

❖

Tin was in agony as was the man loved by her best friend. Both their brothers had been charged and incarcerated, each about to serve an identical prison term of six years. In light of this development, Chew Yong had planned to delay his overseas posting. He had also sought Molly's understanding on postponing their wedding. In fact, she would have suggested the same if he had not even broached the subject.

Besides, what she and Chew Yong mostly talked about thereafter seemed to gravitate towards how best to help mitigate the charges levied against Ming Hao by seeking various legal avenues. Discussing anything else especially their wedding would certainly make them feel less worthy of themselves as caring loved ones let alone decent human beings. On days when Mona's suicidal instincts got the better of her, Chew Yong had to stay home to watch over her which meant time away from Molly. But being a pathological optimist, he held on to the hope that something positive would come their way soon and tried his best to devote his attention to Molly whenever he could afford the bandwidth. Things they used to enjoy doing together like walks in Botanic Gardens, sharing a cone of ice cream, or laughing in a carefree manner over the silliest of topics were now put on the back burner.

Of Tin, Molly saw even less. Since the happening, Molly rarely had the chance to speak with her even though they were living next door to each other. No longer did they spend their evenings lying on a mat in the field and chatting till darkness enveloped the sky. Tin seemed to have retreated into her own cocoon. *She's probably too embarrassed by how it had all turned out between her and Ming Hao—fellow villagers had been calling her a simpleton for not being able to distinguish between a real and a not-so-real man—to talk about the matter, and she's undoubtedly been beaten to flinders with regards to Bok Koon's imprisonment*, Molly kept justifying to herself, troubled by her friend's reticence.

The truth was Tin had not been hiding from Molly or anyone in particular; she had been busy hatching a plan to free both Bok Koon and Ming Hao which would in turn steer Molly's and Chew Yong's wedding back to fruition.

Ah Sokh was a fat man in his late forties with deeply recessed eyes, a flabby chin, wiry black hair, and he talked in a rambling monotone so softly that many would have to strain their ears just to follow what he was saying. The point is, if you were to ask his two wives and eight children how long it had taken them to adapt to his manner of speaking, they would tell you it was nothing short of an ongoing assimilation. As the chief warden of Singapore Outram Prison, he lived in a three-storey mansion next to the prison with a courtyard the size of a paddy field.

He had since taken a prodigious fancy to Tin following a chance encounter with her during his meeting with Gau Pee, yet another of the many failed matchmaking arrangements set up for the latter, and had thereafter indicated to the matchmaker his interest in making Tin his third wife with the assurance that if she were to marry him, her family would not have to worry about money for the rest of their lives. He was then informed by the matchmaker about having to wait a bit longer as Tin's mother had made it clear this nuptial could only take place after Gau Pee's wedding in deference to the Chinese tradition whereby younger siblings would often have to wait for the older ones to tie the knot before they can do so themselves unless the parents chose to intervene or it

had been proven over a reasonable time—anything from two
to ten years depending on the parents' perspective—that the
older siblings were simply not of marriage potential.

'In that case, I may have to wait forever,' said Ah Sokh to
the matchmaker. 'I think the chance of her older sister finding
a husband is as good as dead!' He chuckled, but awkwardly
and a beat too late, a distinctive aspect of his laughter.

This morning, however, his concern about having to wait
forever was put to rest. Sitting across from him in the living
room of his mansion, grand and ostentatiously furnished,
was Tin. She was paying him a visit on her own without her
mother or the matchmaker by her side. If Ah Sokh had not
had a full breakfast, he might have fainted in surprise seeing
Tin at his doorstep following his servant's announcement
that he had a visitor.

'I will marry you any time you like, even before my older
sister gets married,' said Tin, a crackle of nerves plainly
audible in her voice.

'I can't tell you how surprised and happy I am but . . .
what about your mother? She obviously wants your sister to
be married first,' said Ah Sokh softly in his monotone.

'Um, I think she will have no choice but to give her consent
because what I'm about to ask of you will probably supersede
her original condition,' said Tin, her underwhelming tone at
odds with the alpha sentiment of what she was saying.

At this point, Ah Sokh's two wives came into the living room
and introduced themselves, both more or less about the same
age as their husband, the slightly older one rather homespun in
terms of appearance, the other rail-thin and quieter by nature.
The most glaring part, though, was the lack of connubial
tension since it was no secret to them that their husband was in

the process of looking for a third wife. No hint of jealousy, no masked hostility, just empathy, although Tin noticed a deliberate, practised quality to the first wife's friendliness, or perhaps it may have something to do with her bucktooth.

'What do you mean?' asked Ah Sokh whose old-world manners coupled with his roly-poly deportment seemed to serve like amulets against casual indecorum which made Tin hesitate momentarily about what she was going to tell him. But she saw no point prevaricating, knowing that once you pass a point where you could not get to the core of what you really want from the other person, then you probably end up winding round each other in tedious manoeuvres.

'As you may know, my brother and his . . . uh . . . friend are now locked up in your jail and I'm hoping you can set them free based on their good behaviour during incarceration . . . uh . . . once we decide to be married. I'm hoping you can do this for my family. Please, I'm begging you.'

Ah Sokh cocked his head, quietly observing Tin's sombre yet resilient countenance.

'I mean they didn't kill or steal or inflict harm on anyone, they just merely, uh, got on the wrong side of the law,' said Tin.

'What kind of crime have they committed?' Ah Sokh inquired. At first, Tin thought he was trying to make things difficult for her by pretending to be clueless about the whole episode based on her assumption that a warden should always be aware of every crime committed by every person to be locked up in his prison. However, his intense gaze and that sincere flourish of his to want to hear her answer suggested otherwise.

'They were . . . uh . . . intimate with each other,' replied Tin, suddenly awash in plaintiveness as if someone were

choking her yet it seemed the outcome of her own life as
well as that of Bok Koon and Ming Hao depended on her
getting those words out.

'Oh.' Ah Sokh cocked his head again, this time in plain
surprise. 'Are you serious?'

She nodded and said, 'I'll promise to do anything you
want as long as you're able to pull your weight which I'm sure
you can. Please help me, help my family.'

The two wives appeared speechless after Tin's disclosure
of the type of crime committed although you could tell they
had sympathy for her just by looking at their facial expressions.
Ah Sokh was silent too, his thoughts apparently roaming far
and wide. After several minutes, he stood up and walked
around the table to the side where Tin was seated.

'Let's get married,' he said, his reassuring hand on her
shoulder, a strong comforting pressure, like an anchor letting
her know that everything would turn out fine. From that
point onwards, Tin reckoned beyond that chunky body,
those slightly yellow teeth, with curdled coffee breath, was a
magnanimous man on whom she could henceforth rely and
learn to shower her affection and whose priority for family
over other matters she was indeed thankful for. Not only did
he free Bok Koon and Ming Hao immediately, but he also
promised to move Tin's family out of their shoebox unit in
Lorong Limau into a newer and more spacious single-storey
house in Outram. But, in the end, it was just not meant to be

In the space of a few weeks after Ming Hao's release from
prison, Molly and Chew Yong finally got married and moved
to Germany thereafter where the latter was to pursue further

studies via scholarship. Before she left, Molly spent her last few evenings with Tin resuming their daily meet-up in the open field, fully aware that they may not get to see each other again for many years to come.

'If not for what you've done, I doubt I would be able to tie the knot with him under those difficult circumstances,' said Molly in a clipped voice. She commended her best friend for her selfless, altruistic act, for putting the needs of others ahead of hers, for making sacrifices that might have impugned her own destiny. So did the rest of the villagers, showering her with admiration and praise wherever she went, especially Mona and Chew Yong who had helped spread the word of Tin's selflessness and elevated her to some sort of heroine status in Lorong Limau. Mona even went to the extent of prostrating herself in Tin's presence during one random encounter, vowing aloud she would repay Tin's great deed, God willing, if not in this lifetime, then certainly the next.

As for Ming Hao, he managed to politely ambush Tin when the latter was heading out from home to do marketing one morning. Unshaved, wild of coif and not exactly steady of eye, he apologized for not being truthful to her from the beginning and clarified that he had never meant to hurt her.

'I know you may look at me like I'm a deviant, a carrier of some mental disease or as what some people have been saying, an incomplete man, but to me this is as natural as breathing and I can't even explain why I feel and act the way I do,' said Ming Hao, slightly nervous yet never more illuminating in terms of clarity. 'I hope one day you and many others will be able to understand that I don't get to choose to be who I am. I swear I've been drawn towards my own kind since I was a kid as far as I can recall. I would tend to notice boys more than girls, you know, the way they look, what they're wearing, what they're saying.' For the record, he had sputtered more words here than Tin had ever heard coming out of his mouth in any single evening spent with him in the past. He even came across as being effusive, the knots of his repressed fearfulness perhaps finally loosened.

Tin said nothing but simply nodded to show her empathy.

'I can't help it if I like men.' Instead of getting the shudders, it was relieving not to mention cathartic for her to hear someone speak directly about what most people under those specific circumstances would tie themselves in knots to avoid. He also admitted the prospect of his future terrified him utterly. Tin could of course relate to this bit since she herself would not know what to expect from her impending wedding to Ah Sokh, how she would be eventually treated by his wives and children, the role she was expected to play in that household.

Incidentally, he did not mention Bok Koon but hinted at their game plan, that 'we will probably follow Chew Yong to Germany after our studies and take it from there'. Tin assured him there were no hard feelings and wished him all the best. They hugged for the first time, both in tears, trying to reconcile with how they were feeling in that moment.

Back in Tin's household, everyone felt relieved and happy that Bok Koon had been freed with the exception of two persons: Gau Pee who could not care less about her brother and Tin's father who reproached his son for causing him shame and for not being the man he was supposed to be. Every now and then, he would bawl derisive remarks ('Gan-ni-na, tell me now where I am supposed to hide my face? I don't want a jellyfish as my son! I would gladly exchange you for Ah Hock any time!') which would careen off the walls of his house and bounce against its cement floor, his declamation rippling through every syllable as his voice rose by the octave; so ear-splitting was he that neighbours living five or six units away could vividly hear what he was shouting. In hindsight, this might have been the part that could have altered the course of fate if only Tin's father had managed to rein in his mockery.

Other than that, Tin's family was generally in high spirits anticipating their imminent change in financial status vis-à-vis Tin's wedding to Ah Sokh with the exception of Gau Pee yet again who felt utterly sore that her younger sister would soon have a husband ahead of her—Tin's mother had pretty much forfeited the right to insist that Tin could get married only after Gau Pee had done so since the former had in fact made a personal sacrifice to guarantee her brother's release from incarceration—and more so for the fact the husband was the same person who had previously mowed down her own possibility of a future with him the same way he would have swatted a fly with a roll of newspapers. The only comfort not to mention face-saving grace she could bring to herself was to lie to outsiders that her sister would be marrying one of her matchmaking rejects.

Needless to say, she had also been feeling terribly upset over Molly's nuptials, an irredeemable chapter of her life that she would gladly forget. She did not attend the wedding, nor was she invited. Secretly, she wished they would die in a plane crash on their way to Germany.

Although the people in Lorong Limau would always remember her as evil incarnate, she did find redemption later in life for taking care of her mother after the latter contracted tuberculosis—unmarried daughters were expected to stay with their parents till kingdom come, a period of fourteen years spent bathing her, washing her soiled clothes, cooking for her, nursing her poor health, and finally managing her funeral and making sure she was given a respectable send-off.

In the half-light of the candle, they saw his body hanging from the ceiling via one of the ropes used in the recent flood to help Tin's family navigate the waters inside the house. Screams ensued, shadows gouged petrified faces, everyone became harum-scarum. As Bok Koon's slim frame hanged motionless, silhouetted in the light from the candle, it was a case of suicide writ large.

Unable to stomach his father's ceaseless taunts and too ashamed to face a gossipy, judgemental public, Bok Koon chose to take his own life and break his pact of going overseas with Ming Hao, the meaning of his existence already shrunken to gnat-size long before his arrest, a speck of dust he felt that was nowhere visible to the human eye, troubling, worthless. *Ending it would be the right thing to do*, he justified to himself ad nauseam.

Indeed, Tin's family could be jinxed, according to the villagers in Lorong Limau, for their two sons had died young, one after the other in the same year. They wondered if Tin's parents might have committed something abominable in lives past so much so that it had come back to haunt them in the present.

Because of Bok Koon's passing, Tin had to postpone her wedding to Ah Sokh until one hundred days after the funeral, nothing anyone could do except to honour a customary practice. Besides, Tin's family was too traumatized to even sit down together for a meal let alone plan a wedding ceremony. Tin's father went nuclear on those who dared speak ill of his family; Tin's mother was largely bed-ridden for weeks; Kee Kee promised not to fantasize about her gilded future at least not until her mother was back on her feet again; Tin bemoaned her lack of willpower to approach Bok Koon after her first few attempts at initiating a heart-to-heart dialogue with him had been vehemently dismissed; since Gau Pee had never really liked Bok Koon, she forced herself to appear downcast if only to avoid looking awkwardly at odds with everyone else in the family especially in the presence of fellow villagers.

Ah Sokh understood why the wedding had to be postponed but was not too pleased about it. On his end, he could only wait for the hundred days to be over before preparing for the banquet and sending out the invitations. However, the wedding turned out to be a non-entity as he and his entire clan were killed midway through the mourning period by a fire that had immolated his mansion and parts of the prison of which he was in charge. Due to overcrowding, the inmates had accidentally caused a whole slew of lit candles—while marching from one of the narrow hallways to their respective cells—to tumble onto a large canvas covering the walls of an adjoining room thereby triggering an unstoppable fire. Half the guards and inmates were killed as well, the left wing of the prison entirely burnt down.

Once again, Tin's family became the target of condolences, gossip, and wild speculation in Lorong Limau following the fire breakout at Outram Prison and the resulting cancellation of Tin's wedding. 'Oh, that poor girl, my heart breaks for her . . . I think she will grow mentally unstable having to stomach back-to-back tragedies . . . my guess is she might have something to do with the fire, since I've been told she doesn't love him and only used him to free her brother.'

For now, Tin could only sit by herself on the field—since Molly was no longer in the country—and let the hypnotic buzz of the fireflies dull the pain within her, telling herself repeatedly that sometimes you have to let time carry you past your troubles.